W0013868

THE MYSTERY
OF THE
KINGFISHER BOX

by

George Moor

JOHN CALDER · LONDON
RIVERRUN PRESS · NEW YORK

This edition first published 1983 in Great Britain by
John Calder (Publishers) Limited,
18 Brewer Street, London W1R 4AS
and published 1983 in the USA by
Riverrun Press Inc.,
175 Fifth Avenue, New York, NY 10010

The Mystery of the Kingfisher Box

ISBN 0 7145 3973 2

Photoset in North Wales in 11/11 Baskerville by
Derek Doyle & Associates, Mold, Clwyd.
Printed and bound in Great Britain at
The Camelot Press Ltd, Southampton

THE MYSTERY OF THE KINGFISHER BOX

INTRODUCTION

For a year I had been living in Croydon at a teachers' hostel
while I took an intensive course in Chinese. Now that the
course was completed, to get my finances healthy again I
wanted a post as soon as possible. An interim one would do
fine while I fumbled to some decision about my future
career.

I read and re-read the small-lettered advertisement
under 'Miscellaneous' at the back of *The Times Educational
Supplement*. I think it was the word 'restful' that held me
after so much frantic Chinese.

'Tutor — wanted — for frail fifteen-year old boy for "O"
levels. Restful surroundings; own accommodation; country
house Norfolk. Apply Wilming, Vrede Manor, Near
Lytton.'

I brooded, looking for snags. There are not more sharks
even in the City or publishing than there are in education.
But the lad was declared to be frail — a good omen.
Without health he was unlikely to oppose instruction.
Norfolk, where I had never been, I pictured as somehow
bright and breezy — a bracing county with windmills,
hares and gentlemen in hunting jackets visible in the lonely
acres. I saw myself taking the frail pupil, perhaps wheeling
him out on nature rambles through a Constable landscape,
while I sampled the Norfolk ale in a quiet country hostel ...

So I wrote an application and four days later I opened a
reply. The letter had 'FROM MISS WILMING' printed at
the top and it had been written in a sloping angular hand
with a steel nib. Even the ink looked brown and faded so
that only the date, contemporary enough, assured me that I
was not gazing at a specimen of calligraphy in a museum. I
was fascinated. Could Miss Wilming be a retired Mistress
of Girton or a lady-novelist who had hit the jackpot? At all

events anyone who wrote in brown ink and with such a distinguished slope must be a gentlewoman and preserve certain standards. I was prepared to be employed by her and she was prepared to employ me — after (she prudently wrote) she had received satisfactory replies from my referees.

On reading that, I was uneasy lest Nicky and Bill should have used a tone of levity in their replies, and how I wished now I had referred Miss Wilming instead to the Reverend Doctor Lavater, my last headmaster. Indeed I still owed Nicky two pounds ten and could only hope he was not vindictive.

Later I learnt from him that he had written two pages on me as a model of all the virtues; and a registered envelope came from Miss Wilming enclosing ten pounds in cash and bidding me appear at Vrede Manor.

CHAPTER ONE

I did not know when I entered Norfolk. The gradations of the English counties are imperceptible so that only at a point inside a county can one sometimes exclaim of a scene or building, 'This is characteristic!' Then, on entering a new job and part of life, I had ceased to be romantic and nowadays lacked even a modest excitement. In fact I was gloomily wondering whether I had made a mistake in accepting the ten pounds and thereby enlisting under Miss Wilming. Morosely I suspected my own judgment, remembering the time when I had departed for Saudi Arabia (again by introduction of an ill-fated advertisement in *The Times Educational Supplement*) and found myself among head-chopping Muslim fanatics.

But Miss Wilming had the handwriting of a lady, I strove to reassure myself, and Norfolk, or at least Lytton, could not possibly vie with Saudi Arabia in inhospitality. No place on earth could.

There seemed to be a great many hedges and I changed trains twice before at last I was seated in a small train, drawn by a steam locomotive, that would stop at Lytton.

The sun had come out and Lytton with its cobbled square surrounded by a coaching inn, bow-windowed little shops and a stone guildhall had such a clean cheerful and English quality that my anxieties died away and I began to feel a zest for my new adventure. This was a part of England that one could love. I watched the people, unhurriedly greeting each other.

I enquired of the young policeman in the square about the next bus going past. The next one would be leaving in four hours time, so he advised me to take a taxi. Lytton did not look big enough to last me four hours so, appreciating now why Miss Wilming had sent me ten pounds, I followed his advice. The car, for after the London taxis it seemed a mere car, was soon among fields and giant trees in the last green of summer. Forty minutes later we began to pass a high wall on the other side of the road. The wall, overhung in places by ivy and tall trees, was of pale stone and topped by glittering glass set in cement. They must have spent days smashing cellarfuls of old bottles to spike this considerable stretch of wall.

Then the taxi set me and my luggage down before the lodge and iron gates of Vrede Manor. I had brought some records with me, though I was without a gramophone, and I did not fancy the unneeded exertion of carrying the stuff from the Lodge to the house. But as no one came to open the gates, despite my driving in the big white eye of the bell, I let the taxi go and stood there, a little foolish, feeling thirsty and listening to the birds.

'Hold your horses,' called a big fellow appearing with a bucket when I pressed again. 'I was feeding the hens at the back. What do you want?'

'Miss Wilming is expecting me.'

He surveyed my luggage and me and said as a concession, 'I'll open the side then.'

The main gates had on a chain and lock and looked as if they had never been opened since the Prince Consort died. I didn't want to ruin my records and it seemed at first as if my bag would never get through the side gate. However, it just squeezed past, shivering some flaking rust.

'You can leave that here and someone will fetch it,' said the lodge-keeper and reflecting that the bag was soundly locked I set off for the distant house. If a tip had been expected it still was.

I went over a cattle-grid and though no livestock were in sight the stiff lace of dried dung indicated their existence. As the path went between stretches of bracken some fallow-deer flew through the air and into the green again.

The house on a slant lay before me. I had not thought to look up Vrede Manor in an architectural reference book, but clearly it had been designed by an eminent hand in the late seventeenth or eighteenth century. The building was long and looked low though in fact behind the elaborate steps leading down to the extravagant terrace would be a cleverly masked ground floor of kitchens and servants' rooms. The chief wonder for me, however, was that a miniature palace of this type was not in the hands of the National Trust or a local council. Perhaps Miss Wilming was an American?

I wondered, too, how I should approach the house. To ascend those steps from the terrace would be like something from a megalomaniac's dream or an avant-garde French film.

But (shades of Jane Eyre!) to seek the tradesman's entrance would be an insult to private tutorship. Might there not be a neutral, a middling, door? For poor parsons, tutors and governesses.

The house lay in the afternoon sunshine like a stone ship anchored in the park. Sparrows twittered in the old lead gutters and birds sang out in the park, but on the vast terraces nothing moved. The stone bowls that held no flowers were hot to my hand. The bowl of the huge fountain was dry. Looking up at the edifice of stone was like confronting a pyramid, and for all the life visible at Vrede Manor it might have been tenanted by the mummified dead.

There were two worn statues on one of the terraces, with still legible names — Hyperion and Luna: I felt as if I were on the terraces before the mansion of the moon. A front door, like the entrance to St. Paul's, could be seen at the top of the steps but it looked too intimidating for use. I made my way in an arc right around the house, and was glad I had done so for at the back of Vrede Manor was a somewhat less classical façade with a genuine front door and a motor-car just driving away.

The door was opened to me by a butler who must have been aware of my approach before I even knocked. I waited in the cool dim hall while he went to let Miss Wilming know I had arrived. I could smell not the oldness of the house exactly but the smell of polish which is used in old country houses, a smell as of old leather bindings, and blending with this was a more recondite odour, the spice-wood perfume which in sachets was put with priestly Chinese robes for storing. But how had such a sharp fragrance come to an old country house in Norfolk?

As Skinner, the butler, led me to Miss Wilming in the music-room I was partly answered. The rooms I may say were not connected by a corridor but led direct from one into another. But this struck me less than the plethora of Chinese *objets d'art* everywhere. In fact all the furnishings were Chinese, excepting perhaps the silk on the walls and that too could have been Chinese in origin for all I knew. No attempt had been made to simulate a Chinese arrangement of the objects, but such a quantitative assemblage of Chinese things outside the oriental department of a museum was remarkable. I was mystified.

Then I found myself alone with Miss Wilming, who was seated in a silk-stretched French chair. Even here, as well as the grand piano and harp, there was a koto as well as some Asian musical instruments unknown to me.

Miss Wilming explained that the doctor had just visited my pupil-to-be. Perhaps there would be a chance for me to meet him that evening.

About sixty, with greying hair and cold grey capable eyes Miss Wilming indeed reminded me of a principal of a Cambridge girl's college. She spoke softly and very much to the point. Naturally I learned nothing personal about her and I went off escorted by the butler to my quarters as if I had just been interviewed by God in a grey silk dress and neat low-heeled shoes.

I thought I might pump Skinner for a little information but with a head as bald as Anselm of Canterbury's (with a clerical fringe on the circumference) and a Julius Caesar profile he was not a man to encourage confidences. On my directly commenting upon the ubiquity of Chinese articles at Vrede, however, he observed that 'Miss Wilming's ancestors had lived much in the Far East.'

And plundered it much too, I thought to myself. I did not want to shock Skinner by saying so, but he seemed as shocked as if I had when I asked — quite politely — for a cup of tea.

'Tea is at four, sir,' he reproved me. I noticed that I had facilities for making tea in my quarters and made a mental note to buy a packet of Typhoo when I ventured outside Vrede — and a crate of Guiness.

As it was my first day I was summoned at five-to-four to take tea with Miss Wilming in the library. I was comforted to see that tea was not confined to the beverage.

Miss Wilming was as detached, impersonal and soft-spoken as before. I found it impossible to reach into any recesses of her nature or make any human contact beyond politeness. I suspected that she had no sense of humour and felt that this could have accounted for her ponderousness. She did not seem to be particularly happy despite the evidence of wealth about her. Of course there was no reason why she should be. But I found myself hoping my pupil, despite his weak health, might prove livelier.

She referred to him as 'Philip' and once, later, as 'my nephew'. Then she corrected herself — 'My second cousin's son, to be exact. He is the last of the English Wilmings'.

It was at this point she noticed that the French bronze clock on the white marble mantle-piece had stopped. She rang the bell.

'Skinner, the clock has stopped,' she remarked and the butler, looking suitably contrite, extracted a key from inside the back of the clock and wound it up under his mistress's critical gaze. The tick when it came sounded as momentous as a transplanted heart beginning again.

I was impressed by this incident which reminded me that I had now entered a milieu where ladies did not attempt such strenuous activities as winding a clock.

I was not greatly enlightened by hearing my pupil described as 'the last of the English Wilmings', but at least I now knew his name. At eight o'clock I met him for the first time.

On the upper storey I was glad that there was a corridor, except in the Long Gallery. I think the corridor had been added after the original construction of the house, but its existence meant that one did not have to go through a series of private rooms to reach a particular room, as on the lower floor. So I was able to leave my small self-contained flat, which was fully as comfortable as the advertisement had promised, and go past the nursery and schoolroom to the rooms occupied by Philip Wilming.

He was a small dark lad, brown-eyed, and he was listening to pop-music on L.Ps when I entered. I noticed the stereo loud-speakers with relief; the harp in the music room downstairs had suggested rainy evenings when Miss Wilming would sing 'Ombra Mai Fu' to it. Philip looked and sounded lively enough — though perhaps a little 'porcelain' for an English lad. He had the delicate bone-structure of a Japanese. I had taken his aunt's 'frail' as indicating ill-health, and the doctor had called, I knew. But I did not like to enquire the nature of his illness in case it was serious.

He told me he was learning the guitar. Miss Wilming had told me not to stay long and I had intended only a brief call but what with the records and Philip's talking of his 'folk-music' heroes, most of whom I hadn't heard of, an hour must have passed. Suddenly the lights snapped on — for the dark had set in and neither of us had risen to dispel the gloom. Miss Wilming stood there, looking severe.

'Mr. Catlow, I am surprised at you keeping the boy up so late when he has been ill. Philip, with your kidneys you know you must avoid excitement.'

I fled, wondering what affected Philip's kidneys so that at fifteen years of age he could not stay up till nine o'clock. As I shut my door, I could hear her haranguing him, the soft voice not lacking its steel. She probably disapproved of pop-music anyway.

The next morning Miss Wilming sent word that I should start lessons with Philip but be careful not to attempt too much on the first day. Even without her instructions we would hardly have advanced very far when I had yet to find out what stage Philip had attained. In the days following I had evolved a routine and I was very careful to look out for signs of fatigue in Philip and respect them. I was not convinced from the evidence of my own eyes, that Philip had to be treated as an invalid but I assumed that Miss Wilming was relying on a medical diagnosis, and that could not be gainsaid.

Watched by his aunt, Philip never took exercise apart from walking in the shrubberies with me, and after a month at Vrede the bathroom mirror told me I was getting fat. I had no trains to rush for and was under no necessity to go haring out to shops or launderettes. All I did was mildly tutor and eat. I had never felt nor been so inactive in my life. Even a game of rounders would have been a welcome invigoration, but I could not suggest such a thing to the dignified Skinner and I did not know if the state of his kidneys and Miss Wilming allowed Philip to participate in such wild exertions. So I explored the park and the house on foot as much as possible. One seldom encountered Miss Wilming in a posture of locomotion; I think the sight of her possessions wearied and bored her.

'Well, I must say the young fellow's looking a lot better these days,' Mrs. MacDonald, the housekeeper, remarked one day. 'He hasn't wet the bed since you came, either.'

'Wet the bed!' I exclaimed.

'Oh yes — flooded it every night. Mind you, don't go repeating my words, but it had Miss Wilming worried. Had the doctor called in. He's allowed only one cup of tea a day, as you've no doubt noticed.'

'No, I hadn't. And there's nothing wrong with his kidneys or heart — apart from the bed-wetting?'

'No — just his nerves. His mother abandoned him, and that would upset him, stands to reason, the poor duck.'

Mrs. MacDonald, clearly, was my informant in the household. She had been born within the sound of Bow Bells (as she often mentioned, unnecessarily, since her speech proclaimed as much) and her husband, in insurance, had hailed from the Isle of Skye. Left without insurance by the over-optimistic MacDonald, his widow had to return to service.

The staff at Vrede stuck me as numerous in an age of selective employment taxation. The only time when I saw the combined household was on Sundays when by a polite coercion we gathered for a Church of England service in the little chapel that stood apart from the manor. I never saw the gate-keeper in the congregation. Perhaps he was on duty or belonged to another denomination. The staff at Vrede Manor seemed large enough to man a small light industrial factory.

I knew the table-maid who set out lunches and dinners for Philip and me in the old nursery, since Miss Wilming ate alone as much as possible, and from Mrs. MacDonald I had heard of the cook, her friend. Mrs. MacDonald found Skinner stand-offish. But the other servants who appeared at church were unknown to me. I had not set foot at all in the lowest floor of the house, and, of course, an army of people could have been dusting and moving forward through Vrede while someone following never caught up with or saw them or suspected their airy presence. Despite such ample evidence to the contrary, Vrede felt uninhabited, and the reason was that there was enough space for the inhabitants to be out of sight of the others.

Philip's bed-wetting did not surprise me — a timid boy who had been through emotional tension would feel keenly the isolation of Vrede. Miss Wilming would have a doctor attend Philip as she had Skinner wind the clock.

In any case, her elderly influence was unlikely to encourage young male adventurousness. I could not help thinking that there were more basic things which Philip needed to gain than his 'O' levels, such as a sense of security in himself and the confidence of joy.

CHAPTER TWO

Most days Philip and I had tea with Miss Wilming, the only time usually for me to meet her, and afterwards we went upstairs, but only to collect a cricket bat and ball and after a decent interval go out. The early Autumn was too beautiful and sunny to be lost entirely on text-books, and for exercise I felt Philip as well as myself were not a pair of Jane Austen heroines to be contented with a saunter in the grounds. I would keep the cricket-bat against the side of my leg till we were out of sight of the house.

Our meals were usually set for us by a pleasant young girl, Anne Gibson, though from time to time Mrs. MacDonald would come to see us. I was glad that Mrs. MacDonald was not in regular attendance for, though I had welcomed her confidences at the beginning, I thought she was too inclined to gossip and foresaw awkwardnesses if I encouraged her. I appreciated that Skinner was wise in his aloofness, for Mrs. MacDonald would be as inclined to chatter to Miss Wilming about us as she was about Miss Wilming to us. So after the first confidence I was glad not to be on too close a footing with the housekeeper and enjoyed the guileless presence of pleasant Anne at our table, considered her as a possible bowler but reluctantly did not augment our team. Anne's departure with us and a cricket-bat into the park was likely to be thought 'not cricket' at an establishment like Vrede.

After dinner, if the weather was splendid and lessons had progressed satisfactorily, we would sometimes slip outdoors again and enjoy the last of the sun either in strolling and using our cameras or practising with the bat and ball. Philip looked healthier, and there were plenty of winter-months ahead for swotting. It was pleasant to hear him laugh. His face, neck and arms had soaked up the sun.

On our excursions about the park I noticed that what had originally been the east gate had long been walled up but that the west gate was still in use and led to a farm. By this gate the cattle entered and left the park, and after dark it was kept locked like the main entrance.

Every night Skinner walked with a torch through the house to make sure that the security arrangements were in order. Vrede Manor, as regards contents, was like a Victoria and Albert Museum without glass-cases. Gradually at tea-time from Miss Wilming, and also by dipping into books in the library, I learnt how the Wilming family had originally come from Holland with William of Orange. A branch of the family still lived in Amsterdam, diamond millionaires and controllers of the tobacco-empire that produced the famous Wilming cigar. The English branch of the family had done almost as well for themselves, for they had employed to good purposes the revenues which King William gave to Andrea Wilming his friend and had become involved in shipping and trading interests in the Far East. In the nineteenth century the so-called Opium War by which Britain seized ports on Chinese territory had brought rapid expansion and rich opportunities to the shipping firm of Wilming and Osborne. From Victorian times to the days of Miss Wilming's father the younger Wilming males had lived at their residence in Hong Kong, returning to retirement at Vrede only when a more capable son was ready to take over active superintendance of the China trade interests. The opening of Japan had further enhanced trade and there were Wilming and Osborne offices at Yokohama and Kobe through the days when the Mexican dollar was king to the present time of Japan's economic strength. No wonder that as proprietor of one of the largest shippers to Japan and South-East Asia Miss Wilming could still afford the cost of an establishment like Vrede.

Each wave of Wilmings retiring from activity in Hong Kong would wisk new shiploads of Chinese art home to Norfolk. The jades, silks, scrolls and lacquer of generations found their resting place here, mixing with native European items such as the English silver and those silk French chairs in which Miss Wilming was usually to be found seated. The name in the advertisement I had not associated with the Wilming of Wilming and Osborne, and had I done so I would not have guessed at the opulence involved. Names esteemed in Penang, Singapore, Hong Kong and Yokohama are not familiar to all Englishmen, and in a way the names of a company take on a reality of their own so that one does not think of them as still being borne by a living family. There is a Mr. Honda, and one is surprised. The Osborne of Wilming and Osborne became extinct in the reign of Queen Anne. Miss Wilming was very much still here.

When it was raining or Philip had a piece of work to be going on with there was pleasurable occupation enough in contemplating one or two of the works of art set in such profusion throughout the house. I had not told Miss Wilming of my diploma in Chinese, since it had not been relevant to my application, and a year's intensive study of the modern National language was just about enough to let one read a newspaper. The chops in red which held the names of the artists in stylised form on the paintings and statues could not be read by me. I learnt, by asking Miss Wilming, there had been no regular attempt to systematize and catalogue the collection. But by judging the quality and style of a work and my making use of the specialist art-books in the library I could sometimes attribute a work to a period or, if the seal was famous enough to be listed, to an individual artist. Of course, in a country with an old civilization like China one could not rule out that the Wilming who first made the purchase of a very old object, had been sold a copy. That mattered not at all to me who delighted in the subdued colours and the materials and the effortless-seeming painstaking skill.

Even with Western art I could never devour a whole exhibition, but for delight would prefer to concentrate on a chosen piece. With a Chinese scroll or porcelain created to be appreciated on its own I had to sample the items singly. Sometimes a slant of light would pick out a scroll so that, though one had passed it many times before, one saw for the first time the faded brown and weak yellow background against which an old Taoist sage in the palest of blue robes was seated. A small wash of umber suggested a mountainside and from it grew, above the sage's head, a spray of Autumn grass in swift brushstrokes of black and dark green. Each time I looked a new detail would emerge — the basket just peeping from behind the sage; the wash of umber below him was a lake reflecting the mountainside. Later still, I admired the loose black cap, and the face, which had at first impressed one by its serene musing revealed, when looked at closely in the thin brush strokes, the long straggling eyebrow hairs of age as well as a pale goatish beard — seeming pale because the black strokes which composed it were so fine. Just by black lines and a wash of light colour the old artists created a whole world of colours. The scroll-painting which at first glance had seemed so economical revealed a richness of detail, such as the hand held in a religiously stylized posture or the sharp toe of the slipper peeping from his robe. The brush-painter had been a master of illusion, but my first gaze like the last impressed me with the sage's simple and deep seeing through all things. From the mountain he was looking through the lake of the world.

On a day of brighter light I noticed that the colour of the sash-fastening was not blue like the robe but a shade of green that had faded. I felt that I would see new things and win a deeper insight into the sage's vision the longer I looked at the picture. But there was no one with whom I could share my interest except Philip and he was far too young to care yet for the crystalization of quietist experience that the Chinese painter had imaged. It was an old man's painting.

Philip naturally preferred items of an ingenious trick or toy nature such as the silver stork standing on a lacquer box. When you pressed a button the stork bent its head and picked up a freshly rolled cigarette. But from Philip I incidentally learnt of the rooms on our floor which were stacked with chests and boxes of articles sent long ago from China and for which there had not been space enough in the house to set out on display. Vrede did not have attics — directly above us was the stretch of flat roof broken only by chimney stacks and surrounded on all four sides by an ornamental stone balustrade.

I may have given an impression of unlimited leisure but this would be misleading. From eight-thirty to tea-time I was engaged in directing Philip's studies, and if after tea we spent the time outdoors that was simply to make use of the sun while we had it and to help the boy in a more important if non-scholastic way. The servants at Vrede had a television, but neither the Wilmings nor myself had one to watch. I infinitely preferred to survey the treasures of art around us at Vrede and foresaw that gloom and rain as the winter set in would not be a hardship to me.

Miss Wilming read the *Daily Telegraph* every day. She told me that she had been so disappointed in the new *Times* that she had switched to the *Telegraph*. I believe she had a radio in her rooms, those mysterious chambers which I had not seen and about which I was curious as I supposed the mistress of the manor would naturally reserve the most beautiful art-objects for her own quarters.

I suppose Philip was well without a television in his examination year, especially as he had delight and exploring interest enough in music, and I for my part was glad to be without television, where relentlessly dominated by the two senses of sound and sight the mind is allowed no recall and, not probing at its own pace, is hurriedly dragged through a seeming of reality without contact so that there is no accruing of genuinely lived experience. Later, in winter leisure, some of the works of art would have time to unfold and flower in me, the silence and solitude of the house providing a perfect climate. There was not enough time at present to investigate those three store rooms on our floor, away to the other side of the long gallery.

At tea-time I found conversation difficult as I minded my ps and qs in the presence of Miss Wilming: to show the curiosity I felt might have been impolite. With the coming of Autumn the park was colourful, but on the terraces I could not help noticing the complete absence of flowers. There was not even a rose-garden at Vrede and this stuck me as very odd. The stone of the terraces was so overwhelming without the contrast of plants. In the house too one never saw bowls of flowers.

One day at tea-time in the course of conversation I commented on this lack of a flower-garden. Immediately I felt I had voiced a criticism of what was none of my business.

'I do not care for flowers,' stated Miss Wilming in her quiet composed way. This was the first time I had heard such a sentiment, and I was startled. One grows up believing that people like flowers by instinct, but there is no reason why this should be so. Miss Wilming was just being honest.

I made no further remark for one could not have avoided offence in disputing the taste of someone who preferred a stark vista of stone and dust where room had originally been provided for beds and bowls of flowers.

I myself wondered whether perhaps she suffered from hay-fever or had an allergy to flowers. Or was I the odd one in finding her lack of liking strange? I had never before known anyone as rich as Miss Wilming, and I should therefore be prepared for surprises.

CHAPTER THREE

I had not yet gone to bed when there came a tap on the outer door. On opening it I was surprised to see Skinner and from his look I saw at once that something dreadful had happened.

'May I come in?' he asked, keeping his voice low, and immediately stepped inside.

He was usually so aloof and under such muted self-control that I was really encountering him for the first time as a human being. There was sweat on his brow, his incipient jowls were flecked with pink and his collar was slewed to one side.

I made the obvious remark as he panted for breath: 'You look as if you've seen a ghost.'

'I've seen something worse,' he stated. 'I'm sorry to burst in on you like this, Mr. Catlow, but I'd like your support and to be a witness. I've 'phoned the police and the gateman. It's the girl — Anne Gibson.'

'What's happened to her?'

'I found her dead. She's committed suicide — hung herself in the chapel. It's dreadful.'

'But she's too young.'

'Yes,' said Skinner.

'Have you told Miss Wilming?'

Skinner took a grip on himself. 'Miss Wilming has a heart condition. I think she's asleep already and it would be inadvisable to pile this on her just now.'

'I don't want the boy to know,' I said.

'Nobody knows yet except you. Let's go downstairs. His light's still on, so tip-toe.'

We went along the corridor past Philip's door as quietly as possible, and reached the entrance hall where the lights were all on.

'I didn't cut her down,' said Skinner opening the door. For a moment all was dark as the cold night air met me, then he switched the outside lights on. 'I came to get you. Well, Mrs. MacDonald would have screamed her head off, as I felt like doing.'

'Do you know what could have made her do it?'

'I can hardly believe she did such a thing,' Skinner said. 'She was such a natural cheerful girl — the last person I would ever have thought of in connection with suicide. Her mother died last week. I'm not going in there again. I had such a shock. I don't advise you to look at her, but perhaps you would turn the lights on inside for the police.'

We had been walking towards the Chapel. The outdoor light above the door had been turned on and already a moth beat around the glass. Skinner gave me his torch and I went inside and brushed the light-switches on.

Anne must have drawn up a bench to stand on. Now it lay where she had kicked it. The rope had been drawn over a beam in the screen before the altar, and her body hung unmoving before the altar and the commemorative stained glass window behind.

I made no attempt to approach: to have seen her face would have made me distraught. I hurried to rejoin Skinner outside. He was walking under the trees.

'Was she in love with someone?' I asked him.

'Oh no — nothing like that. Unless with someone who never knew how she felt. What a waste of a life!' he exclaimed with fierce bitterness. 'If only I'd started locking up the Chapel first instead of leaving it to the last, I might have been in time to stop her. She never gave a hint she was unhappy with us. We don't — how can we — know the inner world of others?'

We walked up and down in silence under the trees. The final rejection in suicide has all the lesser bitterness of those times when one has been judged too hard to sympathize and too ineffectual to help. What judgment of character could we claim if Anne had not been the confident cheerful girl we supposed, and was there not supreme contempt for us and our lack of insight in this despairing going-off?

The night was filled with the isolation of human anguish — a thousand spirit-voices in the dead leaves of the park. Then, beams of light through the mist, the police-cars.

That night Skinner had shown his real face and afterwards I had a friendly esteem for him. At our meals we missed Anne with her sunburnt arms and shy smile, and I winced as Mrs. MacDonald garrulously went on about what The *Lytton Gazette* had written. Because of her Philip learnt of what had happened, but at least he had had no direct experience of the tragedy. I would have preferred him not to know at all.

The winter had opened on a sombre note, unlike the peace I had expected. Afterwards Skinner was reluctant to enter the Chapel, and in my dreams the hanging body against the stained glass window recurred.

At the inquest the only motives suggested for Anne's suicide had been her mother's death and her own homesickness, though the homesickness was only guessed at.

The winter park appeared more desolate than ever. One felt as if Anne's spirit heavy with inarticulate grief was waiting there in the mist.

I rose in the dark and sometimes when the light came it showed mist right against the house as if Vrede were caught in a cloud like a lamasery on a peak.

CHAPTER FOUR

'I don't think your aunt would altogether approve of my nosing in there,' I remarked uneasily to Philip.

'She's not in — and the doors would be locked if she meant people to stay out,' said my pupil. 'Anyway, you're not going to pinch anything.'

'I don't think so,' I confirmed, giving him a startled glance. I forgot at times that he had not been brought up in the secluded world of Vrede and had once attended a boy's school at Ruislip.

We had been working right up to dinner-time — Miss Wilming having gone across the county to spend the day with an old school-friend, Mrs. Stairs. I thought I would have a peep in the rooms storing those items from China not on display. But Philip did not want to accompany me not foreseeing much excitement in looking at more of what was so abundantly about the house.

A brief glimpse at the first room showed me that the articles there had not been taken out of their first wrappings. So I looked in the second room, and was dazzled by part of a screen which was visible. I went in, closing the door behind me.

There were blinds on the windows, and articles were stacked in such a way that outside light would not have entered. What had taken my attention was a four panelled folding screen of exceptional brilliance. A fabric cover had been fastened about the screen but it had been ripped at one corner so that the lacquer and inlay of a lower panel were revealed. I had not wanted to interfere with the wrappings, but the piece of screen already exposed was so breathtaking that I could not resist the temptation and removed the cover, setting it on the floor.

Other screens in the house were sedate, of dark woods.

This one struck me as having an exceptional purpose. Perhaps it had been made for a young bride? A pair of kingfishers were swooping over a silver stream where willows trailed in the water. I had never before seen lacquers of such brightness. The technique was like that of the Japanese masters, but the form of the screen was indisputably Chinese. I took it, therefore, that the screen had been especially commissioned — not for the quarters of a courtesan, as in that case the motifs of flowers would have been more overtly erotic, I felt. Why kingfishers? Mandarin ducks are the symbolic birds of faithful love.

Nevertheless the screen spoke to me of love and love only. Would such brilliant lacquers have been used in any other but an amorous context? A special present for a loved bride? Yet the Western symbolisms — of kingfishers and willows — were unhappy ones.

But for the Chinese artist using those bold and lovely lacquers surely there would have been no tragic associations. Whatever the screen's origin it had been for a festal occasion.

With those mornings of long ago (I could not help reflecting) when the screen stood in a bedroom in China, poor Anne Gibson who had not been a bride was now a part, gone into the past, while the screen still kept existence. These kingfishers still flashed, triumphant above their silver stream.

To see the other side of the screen I moved it forward and went around. This time the moon had arisen and the kingfishers must have retired to rest. I now appreciated the contrast between morning and evening on the different sides of the screen.

But my attention was diverted by what seemed a companion-piece of furniture to the screen. In the same sort of wrapper as the screen had been, the matching piece rested on the floor behind the screen. I took it at first for a small table, and removed the wrapper. Now I saw it was not a table, but what use it had been designed for I could not say. It was like a small lacquer square stool but the lightness of the wood and the finish of the surfaces made it clear a stool was not intended. A box then. But this box lacquered in colour on five sides and in black underneath did not open. I had picked it up. On the under side were four shaped points that acted as legs, and the top was slightly rounded. On that top surface above the silver stream there flew *one* kingfisher. With the top rounded as it was, the box could not have been used as a ceremonial tray. I was mystified. Perhaps, however, the box just did not have a use. It was hollow inside, and something like a piece of wood moved inside as I held the box up.

'Where are you, Mr. Catlow?' cried a voice from the other side of the screen as the door opened.

'Here, Philip,' I answered, coming out with the box.

'What's that?'

'A mystery. You see it matches the screen, but I can't think of any use for it.'

'A foot-stool perhaps,' he suggested doubtfully.

'Rather uncomfortable — one's feet would slide off, and lacquer-work as elaborate as this would be wasted under foot. Of course it could be. I find it a mystery. It's beautiful enough, though, just to be looked at.'

'I bet it opens. Let me try it.'

'Don't break it,' I warned.

He stood there, his thin hands upon the lacquered willows and his dark eyes searching the surface for a catch.

'There's something inside,' he said.

'A piece of wood come unglued.'

'Well, it should open,' he maintained. 'Unless they glued it all together. Or made it to be a puzzle.'

'Perhaps the kingfisher is the answer,' I suggested. 'There are two on the screen, and only one on the box. Is there another box?'

We began to look but nowhere was there any material the same as that which had enclosed the box and screen. There was no kingfisher motif on any other article. Against the wall under the window was a chest that contained three large stone Jizu and a small wooden box containing small brasses of Buddhas and Bodhisattvas. Philip became interested in sorting the brasses. I did not know whether the Jizu were Japanese or Chinese. They were images of weathered stone and represented a Bodhisattva, a merciful and compassionate wisdom who had come to be associated with crossroads and the guardianship of young children. If they had come from Japan, then could the screen and its companion box also be Japanese? But the screen was Chinese-style and the proximity of objects in the room did not mean that they had an origin in common. Everything was all mixed up in the store rooms. Besides, the Jizu was most likely as much Chinese as well as Japanese. There would probably be a monograph on the subject in the library ...

Philip wanted to take the brasses back with him to his rooms and examine them there.

'Bring the box with you if you're so interested in it,' he suggested. Aunt Wilhemina won't mind.'

'I think she well might,' I said reluctantly starting to restore the box and the screen to their wrappers.

'She needn't know. You can put it back later.'

'No, I wouldn't — not without permission. I shouldn't really have come nosing like this, you know.'

'Well, I gave you permission to come in here. I'm her representative when she's not at Vrede.'

'My manners are saved then,' I smiled as we went off with the box of brasses.

Aunt Wilhemina, however, might well have minded for she knew of the screen's and box's existence, so that I was glad I had not gone so far as to remove the box to my rooms.

At tea two days later she brought the screen into the conversation so that I supposed Philip must have mentioned going into the room, to her.

'The screen is of Ming workmanship and my grandmother — Philip's great-grandmother — was especially fond of it. In fact she had it and the cabinet in her bedroom till the time of her death. My mother had them removed to the store-rooms.'

'A cabinet?' I said with surprise, trying not to display the embarrassment which I felt at having pried into the loved possessions of the family's dead.

'It may not be a cabinet. I assumed that it was something in the nature of a cabinet. Isn't it?' said Miss Wilming vaguely.

'It doesn't open,' said Philip.

'Well, Mr. Catlow,' Miss Wilming remarked with a ghost of a smile, 'I am often surprised when I learn the use of some of the Chinese objects. The uses are quite bizarre at times — so unexpected. Sometimes we are asked to lend items to exhibitions, but the cabinet or box has never been on loan that I can recall, so what it is if it is not a cabinet I cannot say. I expect it will turn out to be a Chinese wig-stand or something as improbable.'

There was nothing in what she said to imply displeasure at my poking about in the store-rooms, but nonetheless she must have considered favourite possessions of her grandmother as especial and private — unless there was some other reason — for when Philip went to put back the brasses he found the door of the middle store-room locked. He took back the brasses and kept them in his room. As long as the door stayed locked I was barred, of course, from further sight of the kingfisher screen and its box.

However, a week later, Miss Wilming must have had something like second thoughts for she sent a key to the third room to me by way of Skinner, with a message that she thought I might like to look at the wall-scrolls stored in the room but to keep the room locked when I was not viewing them. I don't know why she had suddenly decided on this precaution, except to exclude curious servants, but I doubt if any of them would have been much interested in the scrolls kept rolled in their long thin boxes like diminutive coffins.

CHAPTER FIVE

As November dragged on I began to feel as if I had been at Vrede for years. Working at the school-subjects and then going for a walk in the bare grounds as exercise had something prison-like about it. Even more so, I was conscious of the gates, now that with the trees so bare one could see to the iron gates and the stretch of glass-topped wall. Philip told me how cellar-loads of old bottles had been broken under orders from his great-grandfather. Now collectors from all over the county would come in the summer to try and find dated pieces of old glass-bottles among the millions of fragments topping the wall.

Vrede in winter had something of the monotony of a Siberian fortress or a tower on the Great Wall. I felt at times like the soldiers on a desolate steppe watching the geese above flying to their warm homelands, and I thought of the despair which had driven Anne Gibson to the Chapel.

If I felt like this, what about Philip, who being younger, no doubt found monotony more destroying? It was time, I decided that we had a day out, a break away from Vrede. But miles out even from little Lytton, where was there for us to go? Even an old gangster film in a Lytton flea-pit, if the place ran to a cinema, would have been a change. But alas! Lytton seemed to have no Odeon or Plaze — just (as the *Lytton Gazette* informed us) bingo in the Old Baptist Tabernacle, and 'The Dream of Gerontius' performed by the students of a college of education.

I was considering this second item as perhaps better than nothing when the reflection came that I would get better value in buying a record by an international company of an Italian opera. Philip and I might have a short excursion and find a record shop in Lytton.

'Oh no, the record shops are in Snortbury,' he told me. 'It's a bigger place.'

I looked Snortbury up in a guide and found that it had been founded by Queen Boadicea's father-in-law, re-established by the Saxons, burnt down by the Danes, and, to quench the heat and thirst of the fire, provided two hundred and fifty public houses and a communal swimming pool. It looked a likely place.

Miss Wilming smiled on our expedition and booked a taxi to fetch us to and from the station at her expense. With plenty of the male staff capable of being chauffeurs, the lack of private transport at Vrede looked at first a little odd. But both her parents had used a horse and carriage to take them about, and Miss Wilming herself had kept on the stables till they had become uneconomic in the nineteen-thirties. From that time she had had a standing arrangement with a taxi-firm in Lytton. Her guests were met by taxi, and had I let Miss Wilming know by what train I was arriving I too in the beginning would have been met by taxi, so Skinner told me.

On a colourless day at the beginning of December Philip and I were driven through the gates of Vrede to take a train from Lytton and a day's shopping in Snortbury.

It was pleasant to have the experience of spending money again. As Christmas was in the offing I bought a few gifts and some cards, for those of my friends who still sent cards to me and about whom I would have felt mean if I had not sent one back. I bought an extra one for Miss Wilming — a horse of aristocratic nose whisking its tail in a thick snowstorm — as this seemed appropriate. Any gift to such a wealthy employer would have seemed trivial. Philip bought a table-lamp with a horrifying orange shade, as a result of which he could not walk more than a few yards without having to put it down and rest, and we were glad to arrive at the dining-room of the Lord Weymouth and have a sit-down for lunch.

The waiter took Philip's table-lamp into his protective custody and I fell to studying the large notice prohibiting the bringing of dogs into the restaurant — a most un-English edict and which worked against the traditional beamed baronial character of the room.

At a table in the corner I noticed a young Chinese man

and woman already at the pudding. Their hair shone blackly like Philip's. In a Western setting it is not always easy to distinguish some Chinese faces from those of other South-east Asians, but as they were about to settle their bill I heard them exchange a few words of Cantonese with each other. They had the becamera-ed air of tourists, though what a season to see England, I thought.

In the afternoon we sallied out to the record shops and Philip bought a Bulgarian record of P.I. Tchaikowsky's 'Liturgy' and another of Stevan Mokranjac's 'Liturgy' while (not to be overshadowed) from the bargain stacks I triumphantly carried away a set of three UNESCO records of 'The Music of Tibetan Buddhism' with an explanatory pamphlet in Japanese. Miss Wilming fortunately did not inhabit rooms directly below Philip's or mine but whenever we later played the results of one day's musical purchases Mrs. MacDonald had a look in her eyes of one under bombardment, as Philip enjoyed music played at full volume.

We spent tea-time in The Kettle and Tinker, Philip having a meat-pie and a bitter-lemon, and we rounded off the day by seeing a Venezuelan film billed as *Forbidden Passion* about a middle-aged sailor who unknowingly commits incest with his teenage daughter in a brothel, in the last scene the pair of them walking together into the sea to die. All the slow Spanish was rather soporific, but the film made a change.

On the way home in the train we suddenly discovered that Philip no longer had the table-lamp which we worked out must still be in the custodianship of that thoughtful waiter at The Lord Weymouth.

CHAPTER SIX

Two days later we were all having tea in the Blue Room, so-called because of the colour of the wall-silk, where the smallness of the room with a fire made one feel cosier than in the library. Miss Wilming was not feeling too well, I think, and the temperature had dropped some degrees so that I had put on an extra pullover and now, so close to the fire, was regretting I had done so.

Had Miss Wilming been ill she would not have summoned us to tea, but her eyes showed fatigue and I suppose the cold weather was a strain on her heart. She was probably feeling a little out of sorts, as she might have said had she confided in us, and so we attempted to maintain as peaceful and relaxed an atmosphere as possible. Her life was solitary enough so that a little human society was no doubt agreeable to her, so long as it did not turn out much of a strain.

But we were interrupted by Skinner. He came to announce that some visitors had arrived at the Lodge gates.

'Visitors?' queried Miss Wilming with both annoyance and surprise.

'A Mr. and Miss Wing — spelt W-I-N-G from Hong Kong. They have given Hitchcock a card. He gave me to understand that they will not be easily deterred from seeing you.'

Miss Wilming had sat back in her chair, her hands on the arms, and closed her eyes.

'Do you mean they would force their way in?'

'No,' said Skinner, 'but Hitchcock said you would be having tea and they replied they could wait. They are in their own Morris eleven hundred.'

'It is most inconvenient,' said Miss Wilming rallying. She sighed.

Skinner now produced a portable telephone seemingly from out of air and discreetly plugged it in.

'Hitchcock,' the mistress of Vrede Manor commanded, 'you may admit Mr. and Miss Wing.' She put down the receiver and spoke to Skinner. 'Bring the visitors in here when they arrive. We shall need extra tea. And Skinner, I want you to stay close in case I have reasons to wish not to be alone with Mr. and Miss Wing — perhaps I am fanciful but ... Anyway, show them in here.'

She maintained her composure but the surface did not hide the anxiety beneath. She now suggested that Philip move to sit at her side before the visitors arrived, and as he did so I perceived that her attitude was protective. Philip's transfer left me more exposed to the fire than ever, so, under the excuse of letting guests from the outside cold have more of the fire, I seized the chance to suggest that I also should move my place.

Miss Wilming nodded indifferently, and I moved to a seat behind the table furthest from the fire. Only Philip went on eating and drinking. Miss Wilming was on edge, and I was as fascinated as if I had been at a play.

I found it incredible that a blackmail attempt should be made on her or that she should ever have done anything for which she could be blackmailed. But I could think of no other reason why she should be frightened and find this visit so evidently distasteful.

By the time the visitors from Hong Kong had been shown in, Miss Wilming was in command of herself again. I was astonished to find myself face to face with the Chinese couple we had already seen in the Lord Weymouth. There were handshakes and introductions all round, though Miss Wilming, I noticed, introduced Philip simply as 'Philip Wilming.'

There were not so many Chinese travelling about Norfolk in the winter for it to be very strange that the pair I had observed at the inn in Snortbury and the Mr. and Miss Wing now calling on Miss Wilming were one and the same.

After the introductions were made Miss Wilming persuaded her guests to be seated.

The visitors were young — at least, Mr. Wing was about

thirty but his lean physique made him appear younger. His sister was in the mid-twenties, and was shy, out of politeness and also from the cold for as she soaked the warmth of the fire she smiled for the first time and her face became less grim.

The conversation was of the most formal and polite nature, as the Chinese were practising with enthusiasm, the type of conversational English which they had studied as the one appropriate to the situation. On the other hand, Miss Wilming was following the convention which custom had prescribed for her. She was the perfect hostess at tea.

What had caused her flurry when she heard of the Wings' arrival was now not in evidence. From the politely smiling and interested Chinese faces one could not suppose them to have more concern than obtaining lemon-slices for their tea and sampling the muffins which, they had read, tasted better in an English winter.

All Philip and I learnt were that Mr. Leong Yok Wing and his sister An Chü were from Hong Kong and had come to England on a matter of business.

For a moment Miss Wilming's eyes had looked pointedly thoughtful, and then with just the right intonation of bright polite concern she swung around to the winter weather which had been distressingly cold so early this year.

I had the sensation of watching a skilled game of verbal ping pong.

But finally there was no more need for muffins or tea.

Miss Wilming began to sing the praises of the English fire in winter, 'on days like this.'

I chipped in with a quotation from Cowper's 'Task', and I sensed that Miss Wilming was grateful for my keeping the subject stirring while she was thinking of something to prolong it further.

She remarked that the winter was not the best of time for travelling but she hoped that while in England Mr. Wing and his sister would find a chance to visit Ely and Peterborough Cathedrals.

'And Winchester' — I put in.

Durham too was well worth a visit, Miss Wilming considered. Though, of course, if possible, Mr. Wing and his sister should try to see something of the Continent, particularly the cathedral of Chartres with its stained glass and stone carvings.

Mr. Wing, speaking perfect English, said that they would very much like a tour through France now that they were on the steps of Europe. But their plans were not so forward. His task in England must be accomplished first.

As he said this, Miss Wilming turned pale, her face having a tortured expression. The conversation died utterly. We heard the sifting of the wood-ash in the fireplace.

What is said can sometimes be of less importance than what is not spoken. During the interchange of remarks Philip had been mostly silent and, apparently, bored. I was aware of the tension between Miss Wilming and Mr. Wing, though the conversation was innocuous enough.

I did not know what Miss Wilming feared, but now as she slumped back pale and silent I sensed that she did not know what to do, how to resolve the situation and get the visitors to go. Against all etiquette but sensing her desperation in her sick look, I intervened in a sympathetic healthy voice. 'I'm afraid that before you came Miss Wilming was very unwell and she will have to return to bed. There is a lot of flu at this time of the year.' And I rang for Skinner. 'Miss Wilming is feeling the affects of flu. Perhaps Mrs. MacDonald can help her to bed.'

The guests were, of course, too well-mannered to remain when the tea-trolley was being removed and the hostess carried off to a sick-couch. Skinner's job required that he have a lot of intuition, though I rather wondered just what intuition of my own had made me take over the captainship from Miss Wilming and ring for Skinner on my initiative. Evidently I had done the right thing, for as she left Miss Wilming said in a low voice, 'Thank you, Mr. Catlow.'

It was Philip and I who took leave of the smiling Chinese guests, expressing the hope that Miss Wilming would soon recover, and Skinner, of course, who accompanied them to the entrance.

I found it a most baffling visit.

CHAPTER SEVEN

For three days afterwards Miss Wilming did not have tea with us. Dr. Gourlay had been called and, as if in punishment for the lie I had told, he found she had flu and recommended her staying in bed. Mrs. MacDonald also caught it, so that Philip and I rather welcomed an isolation which kept us immune.

A young man-servant brought us our food, with Skinner coming along for a spell of supervision when he was free. On one occasion being alone with me, he mentioned that Mr. Wing had telephoned Miss Wilming, but she had asked Skinner to say she was too unwell to answer the phone. Though this was partly true, yet it was more true that Miss Wilming seemed so reluctant to meet the visitors from Hong Kong that she appeared afraid. She had not wished to be alone with them when they called, and now she would not even talk with Mr. Wing on the phone. He and his sister were apparently still at the hotel in Lytton where when we first met them they told us they had put up.

When we did meet Miss Wilming again at tea-time she looked as wan as one would have expected from someone who had suffered from flu. At the same time this made a perfect mask for any anxiety that she might be feeling. She spoke with great naturalness and with more seeming interest than usual, but never once mentioned the Chinese visitors.

She had given Skinner instructions to make sure that the burglar-alarms and warning-devices were in working order and on his last patrol about the house to be sure to carry a revolver. The Chapel was now locked before dark so that Skinner did not have to venture from the house.

Miss Wilming's nervousness communicated itself to me. I did not have a permit to carry a gun as Skinner did, and I would have been more nervous if I had, but I would wake up in the middle of the night as if to assure myself that none of us were being murdered. Was Miss Wilming's fear only for herself, or was she apprehensive of Philip's being attacked or kidnapped? He was alone in his lonely rooms along the creaking corridor, with empty rooms between us and the enormous house around. In the winter nights it seemed more enormous.

I could not press more security upon Philip as I did not wish to alarm him. He had to be spared nervousness. But he locked his bedroom door at night, and there were security-devices on his windows.

After all, I told myself, Miss Wilming, while decidedly not imaginative, is inclined to fuss and exaggerate where danger is concerned. Her reluctance to face the Wings could be due to some quite everyday business complication which had made the Wings feel they had a complaint against the firm of Wilming and Osborne. Miss Wilming would naturally shrink from personal contact with any unpleasantness arising from the activities of the firm. She would not feel responsible for upsets in the firm's day to day running.

The Wings had seemed very pleasant people, though we had not broken the surface formality, and I could well believe that a powerful trading and shipping organization like Wilming and Osborne's had ridden rough-shod over pleasant people in the course of its expansion.

Evidently Philip and I had had our day out in Snortsbury just in time. While the Wings stayed in Lytton and Skinner patrolled the rooms of Vrede with a pistol, I could only suppose that Miss Wilming would not welcome our venturing beyond the safety of the walls. The next break from routine would have to be Christmas, now two and a half weeks away.

I was in bed reading a faded booklet I had taken from the library, a contemporary life, published in Japan, of the Empress Dowager Tz'u Hsi, when there was a knock on the outer door, and I was reminded of the night when Anne Gibson had committed suicide in the Chapel. I opened to find Skinner, still dressed in his daytime clothes.

'There are intruders outside, Mr. Catlow,' he said.

'Have you called the police?' I asked, seeing the gun

Skinner was holding pointed at the floor as if he found it undignified and distasteful.

'That would be premature. I recognized the prowlers as Mr. and Miss Wing. The young lady's figure is unmistakeable.'

'Just the two of them?' I asked, having a vision of the house being encircled by hordes of Chinese like the Boxers about whom I had just been reading.

'So far as I could distinguish, yes,' Skinner replied.

'No alarms have gone off?'

'Mr. Wing seems aware that alarms are likely to be in position. I believe he and the young lady are endeavouring to reach the roof.'

'This is very awkward, Skinner,' I complained. I was a bit tired and I had been getting enjoyably drowsy over my books. Now I was dragged back to decision and thought. However, I realized I should be annoyed with more reason at the Wings, who were responsible, than at Skinner. 'The police are really the ones to tackle prowlers, especially if the prowlers are armed or adept at ju jitsu.'

'It is the notoriety one wishes to avoid,' said Skinner sententiously.

'What side of the house are they endeavouring to scale?' I asked.

Apparently they were ascending the side of the house from which Philip's and my windows looked, but at the far end of the corridor.

'From the right position and angle,' I pointed out, 'with your gun you should be able to pick them off like ducks.'

Skinner was obviously distressed at the very idea. 'We have never had duck, partridge and pheasant shooting here in my time,' he protested. 'I would be averse to winging a young lady clinging to a wall. Perhaps you would be more successful, Mr. Catlow.'

'I?' For a moment I thought he was joking, then I saw from his face that he was not. Swatting a fly was too bloody an operation for me. 'We must try persuasion, Skinner,' I told him.

He looked sceptical, but my mind was now working. I filled a light plastic bucket with water and had Skinner come with me along the corridor to where he thought the Wings were making the ascent on the outside. I asked him to switch off the alarm on the window, and then turn on the lights when I threw up the window.

The window was a large one at the top of the stairs connecting our floor with the corridorless one below.

Half-blinded by the brilliance I hung looking out but could see nothing below but the wall dropping away. Then I turned myself around and looked up. If they were above me, the bucket was useless.

'Miss Wing,' I called out. 'You have been discovered. We are armed. Now will you please get down.'

I was surprised, as was Skinner, at the authority in my voice, but one is not a school teacher in vain.

Miss Wing's voice drifted from above me piteously. 'Oh, I am stuck.'

Her brother called encouragingly to her in Chinese. 'Don't look down.' He was about four feet higher up the wall than she.

'Skinner, the young lady is stuck,' I told him. 'We'll need the fire-brigade to get her down.'

Philip, I saw, had now joined Skinner.

'I think it would be inadvisable to summon the fire-brigade at this hour,' declared Skinner, who plainly preferred to have Miss Wing splattered on the ground below than have a disturbance at Vrede.

'Mr. Wing, will you descend to the ground and we shall attempt to rescue your sister,' I called up to the silhouette against the wall.

'Are you going to rescue her?' asked Philip admiringly.

'Certainly not,' I answered. 'If Skinner can obtain a long ladder quickly, then we can bring Miss Wing down without having another inquest.'

Philip was disenchanted at my not playing a hero's part. But I would never have been able to clamber up the wall anywhere near as high as Miss Wing had done. I marvelled at her and her brother's agility. No doubt they had been in training for this. Fleeting across my brain came the question — what sort of training? As guerillas or cat-burglars?

'We'll soon have you down,' I called up to Miss Wing with lying encouragement.

Skinner and some men-servants were hastening clumsily from the front door with a ladder. They looked rather like a semi-paralysed centipede. Mr. Wing was now standing directly below the window from which Philip and I were hanging out. He looked quiet and abashed.

Mrs. MacDonald in a long coquettish pink nightdress that trailed beneath a superb red robe like a prize-fighter's had also appeared. All the outside lights were on, like a *son et lumière*.

The ladder was extended and set against the wall. Barry, one of the young men-servants, seemed to have taken charge and it was he, fortunately, who ascended the ladder to rescue and bring down the nerve-stricken Miss Wing. Later I learnt that Barry had formerly been in the fire service, from which he had been dismissed for an act of moral turpitude with a female cashier, so the skill and enthusiasm with which he carried down Miss Wing was easily accountable for. His presence was a stroke of luck for I doubt if anyone else of us present there would have had the expertise to balance from the dangerous-looking ladder and, while retaining a foothold, manage to get a firm grip on Miss Wing.

I told Philip to stay upstairs and I left the house to join the group outside. Skinner seemed to have the situation under control and was speaking firmly and politely to Mr. Wing who looked crestfallen and a bit foolish. He had his arm about his sister who had her face against his chest while murmuring, 'Ah Yuk, I'm sorry.'

I did not want to intrude when Skinner was managing so well, but I did ask, 'Have you taken their weapons?'

Mr. Wing smiled.

'I haven't asked,' said Skinner.

'It's not amusing,' I told Mr. Wing.

'But it is,' he replied, and turned out his pockets. He had a flashlight, a bunch of keys on a ring and a packet of polo mints.

'I have suggested that Mr. and Miss Wing, if she is sufficiently recovered, should leave by the route they came,' said Skinner.

'Very well,' said Mr. Wing, adding good-humouredly, 'Our entry was unconventional, by ladder over the wall.'

'You can leave by the gates if you prefer,' said Skinner.

'No, it is a good ladder — a new model, from Hong

Kong,' said Mr. Wing, losing something of his hang-dog air.

I had put a pullover over my pyjamas and my legs felt frozen as we walked down the drive towards the gates. Hitchcock was no doubt sleeping the sleep of a faithful lodge-keeper for there was no light in the Lodge. We turned from the path past the hen-house and walked on the grass near the wall.

Then we saw the ladder, a sort of blue-metal platform extending right over the broken-glass top of the wall, and a light steelmesh ladder dropped from the platform to our feet.

'It all folds up and goes in the car-boot,' said Mr. Wing with some pride.

'It reminds me of the princess' hair by which the hero got into the tower,' I remarked of the light-weight ladder. 'But you could have done with a far larger winding platform to reach the roof.'

Skinner coughed, a gentle reminder not to stand in technical discussion. Mr. Wing shook my hand and went up the ladder.

'Thank you both,' said Miss Wing with a faint smile, and ascended the ladder to be helped at the top by her brother. Then he drew up the light-weight ladder and at the top retracted the platform, waved and disappeared.

We heard the boot slam and the car drive away. We began to stroll back.

'But what did they want?' I asked Skinner.

'To get into the house. The easiest way is from the roof, by that opening over the stairs.'

'Yes, but what did they want in the house?'

'Ah,' was all Skinner answered, a sort of non-committal verbal shrug.

'Didn't you ask?'

'I asked, but they didn't say. I think it was to speak to Miss Wilming.'

'She'll have to know about all this. Everyone was awakened, except her.'

'I'm afraid so, Mr. Catlow,' came Skinner's voice resigned to troubles to come.

CHAPTER EIGHT

In the morning I did not hear my alarm clock and arose an hour and a half late. I wondered why Philip had not called me as I was late for his lesson, then I supposed I must have failed to hear from him. I went to get shaved, but my hands seemed so leaden and my legs and spine so weak — apart from my face looking even more lifeless than usual first thing in the day — that I knew that I had a cold or flu.

When I was reasonably prepared to face others, I went along to Philip's rooms but he was still in bed and asleep. I hadn't the heart to rouse him, as I did not feel up to a lesson and he did not look well. I staggered back to my room, sneezing in the corridor, and rang the bell. I hoped that whoever answered would have the wits to bring up a belated breakfast. I plugged in a kettle of hot-water for tea. I felt as ghastly as I had looked.

'Good morning, Mr. Catlow,' said Skinner chirpily, appearing with a tray of food and looking very clean-shaven and immaculately dressed as if he had been wound up for the part.

I shuddered.

'You look as if you've overslept,' he commented. 'Barry brought a breakfast up earlier but couldn't get in.'

'I think I've a touch of flu,' I groaned.

'You don't look too good. Miss Wilming rose early, and she would like to see you. But probably she won't if she hears you are unwell.'

'She's no doubt passed her flu on to both Philip and myself. He doesn't look well.'

'Shall I put the fire on for you?' asked Skinner fussing over me. 'I'll look in on the young chap. If I may be so bold, it would perhaps be better if you did not see Miss Wilming just yet. She's having the Chief Constable to lunch. The business of last night has terrified her and she hasn't calmed down yet. I have had to give the impression, I fear, that Mr. Wing and his sister made a forcible escape. I did not say so but I let it be implied that my shot went astray. I am having twinges of conscience, what with one thing and another, especially the Chief Constable's coming, but any written statement I have to make will be the strict truth. I fear I shall be found out.'

'But did Miss Wilming want the police called last night?' I asked.

'Far from it,' responded Skinner. 'But she doesn't like the Wings going off scot-free as she expects them to make another attempt. That's what she wants to talk to the Chief Constable about, I expect. With tension in the household may I be so bold as to suggest that Master Philip have his breakfast in here with you? Miss Wilming is all on edge worrying about kidnapping and murder.'

'Well, he's asleep at the moment, but I'll go along to his rooms, then you can tell her you left us together ... Oh I do feel awful. I must take some Phensic.'

'I'll bring the tea for you,' said Skinner thoughtfully. 'No doubt you'd like another cup. The pot is quite full.'

Once in Philip's rooms he switched on the fires. I looked in the bedroom and saw my pupil still lying there in the sweat-faced sleep of influenza.

'I think you had better tell her that Philip has a cold, and ask Dr. Gourlay either to come or send something,' I told Skinner, who did not sigh but maintained the complete composure of his profession. Hard on the heels of sending for the Chief Constable, Miss Wilming was now to learn that the nephew, about whose health she was always so anxious, needed the services of a doctor.

I turned the key in the door after Skinner, then I drained the pot of tea and sat in an armchair by the fire. My head felt full of drifting cloud. It was the middle of the morning but I fell asleep in the armchair.

When I awoke the room seemed full of people. Barry the man-servant was just leaving. Mrs. MacDonald was smoothing down a bed which had not been in the room when I fell asleep in the armchair.

'I poked the key out and used another to get in,' said Skinner apologetically. 'The doctor's with Master Philip now, then he'll see you. Miss Wilming asked if you would stay here with him so I've had a spare bed brought in — If you prefer Master Philip could move into your rooms — but it's up to you and him to decide.'

Mrs. MacDonald withdrew and Skinner suggested I move to the bed as more comfortable. Like a zombie I moved across.

'Miss Wilming has sent you this bottle of whisky and suggests that you take some with hot water and lemon.'

'Very kind of her,' I said.

'And this is for under your pillow,' said Skinner handing me a gun. He did not look me in the eye.

'Does it work?' I asked.

'I believe so,' said Skinner.

I put it under my pillow, but when I lay down I could feel it like a lump if iron.

'Under the mattress would be better,' I complained.

'The idea, I believe,' intoned Skinner, 'is ease of access.'

'It makes me nervous.'

'I quite understand the feeling,' said Skinner soothingly.

Doctor Gourlay, who had a look of Bob Hope, came in. He examined my tongue and the whites of my eyes, then moved his stethoscope over my stomach. I did not deign to argue with him when he told me I had jaundice. If I did not have flu, I knew I had a cold. All my sensations were of a cold. Doctor Gourlay's finding something else seemed irrelevant.

'No butter or fats,' he ordered.

He had pronounced that Philip was running a temperature.

Anyway, if he had forbidden butter or fats, he had not said anything about whisky, so I took a good slug of it and went into a deep dreamless sleep for thirty minutes, with the gun in my shoe at the side of the bed.

I woke to see Philip sitting in his pyjamas and biting a piece of cheese wrapped in silver foil.

'What are you doing?' he asked.

'What am I doing?' I exclaimed. 'I'm guarding you. The question is — what are *you* doing, with that box of cheese?'

'I'm hungry. Could you spare a drop of your whisky?'

'Get a glass,' I told him, eyeing the cheeses. 'I wouldn't mind one of the cheeses.' Then I remembered cheeses were fat. 'What time is it? Surely lunch is about due. I see visions of hot steaming soup ... Has your temperature gone?'

'It's going down, I think ... Would you like some music?'

'Yes, I would. But not the Bulgarian liturgies. Some chansons. They should be good for jaundice.'

'Is that serious?'

'I am forbidden butter or fats. Lunch *is* late.'

'Are you really guarding me?' asked Philip with a candid scepticism that was almost an insult.

'Certainly. I can't help it if simultaneously I have jaundice. That's enough whisky.'

There was a knock on the door and I was glad that Philip had enough nous to conceal his empty whisky glass. Mrs. MacDonald entered with, 'Walking on your bare feet in pyjamas, young man — you'll give yourself double pneumonia! I'm sorry to be a bit delayed with the lunch.'

She felt the impact of 'La Vie En Rose' played at Philip's usual strength and commented, 'That noise won't improve your liver any, Mr. Catlow. It'd give me jaundice.'

'It helps his French,' I said weakly.

'I don't feel so good myself,' she confided as she set Philip's meal at the table and mine on the tray. 'All the upset of foreigners climbing up the walls to come and hack our heads off! I couldn't get back to sleep last night for thinking of it. I just don't know how English people can go into those Chinese restaurants. The dog is man's friend and wasn't made for eating, I say.'

'Please Mrs. MacDonald,' Philip protested, 'we're eating!'

'Talking about dogs,' went on Mrs. MacDonald on her way out but pausing at the door, 'we're going to have a team of them here — those big guard-dogs to prowl the grounds at night. The Chief Constable has recommended it, so I told cook to be saving all the bones in future. As MacDonald used to say, 'What the fool wastes would be his feast in want.'

'I only hope the guard-dogs can co-exist with the fallow-deer,' was Philip's comment to me.

My jaundice must have been a very mild attack, or perhaps jaundice is like that, for I was never aware of it, unlike the cold. Once I was free of the cold I felt fine, but Dr. Gourlay still regarded me as a patient and I was confined upstairs. However, we went on with the lessons, and I fetched a few personal things from my rooms since I was now to be Philip's bodyguard as well as tutor.

The visible result of Miss Wilming's lunch and chat with the Chief Constable was the presence in the grounds each evening of six awe-inspiring German Shepherd hounds like a pack of well-behaved wolves and with them their handler Constable Alan Barr, who had beautiful pink cheeks and a nice touch on the guitar. As he ate in the kitchen, Barr's musical talent was described to me by Mrs. MacDonald.

With our own constable, who may well have been rented by the week, to Miss Wilming, for all I know, six formidable dogs who would have put respect into any sensible intruder, all the burglar alarms and the gun which I kept permanently in one of my unused shoes under the bed, there was a by no means negligible deterrent to a new attempt by Mr. Wing to sneak into Vrede Manor.

The immediate results, however, were that I was under a constant strain lest somebody, including myself, should let the gun off by accident and that Hitchcock the lodgekeeper protested the dogs by running around and barking at night were putting his hens off the lay and wrecking his health. He refused to open the gates for Constable Barr and Skinner had to go to the Lodge, where a most unpleasant scene ensued.

Vrede Manor ended up without a lodgekeeper and for a week Skinner had a black eye and had to wear a glove over his bitten right hand.

CHAPTER NINE

Fortunately Christmas arrived to make a diversion. Miss Wilming was as enthusiastic about having a Christmas tree as I was. We were both rather impatient with Philip who took not the slightest interest in the tree. Indeed he was aggressively bored with the whole business which he condemned as childish, and his aunt and I and Skinner and Mrs. MacDonald could not help feeling aggrieved as he was the young one who was supposed to justify the whole business.

I love the smell of a fir tree in a room and the glitter and flash of thin silvery ornaments. While we were decorating the tree Miss Wilming became more lively and happy than I had before seen her.

What with my jaundice, the dogs in the grounds and Miss Wilming's fear of anything happening the only exercise I had had in the past weeks had been walking in the house. I hoped this state of affairs would not continue into the new year. The Christmas break from routine was all the more welcome.

I felt rejuvenated by the smell of tangerines and the sight of frost-swirls on the windows, probably from some association of childhood memory. I wished Philip could share something of this pleasure in winter. He was rather moody and bored. I attributed this to his having no companions of his own age, to his adolescence and lacking exercise. To remedy the last I set up table-tennis in my old living room. His aunt would never have approved of my taking him skating. With the temperature dropping I expected that the local ponds were likely to be frozen before long. However, table-tennis was better than nothing.

During the days now one of the younger men-servants took charge of the gates and at night Constable Barr made the lodge his headquarters. Early in the new year a married couple were expected to come and take over Hitchcock's old job.

The Wings, I heard from Skinner, had left Lytton for London on the same day that we had found them trying to break in. Miss Wilming had laid no charges against them, but from the measures she had taken she seemed to fear a new attempt on their part to enter Vrede.

The frosty winter sunniness was delightful. In rooms where the central heating had not been switched on there was a tingling stillness, and the colours on an old vase would seem to acquire a new tone. I would have liked to have viewed the effect of this cold wintry brightness on the blue of the kingfishers on the screen, but that would have meant moving the screen to a room with windows facing the terrace and obtaining Miss Wilming's permission. I had not previously thought about it but obviously a changing temperature does affect the materials of works of art. They have, as it were, a life responsive to weather, their days of best condition.

Now that I was sleeping in what had been Philip's study and living-room, we started to use my former rooms as our dining-room and table-tennis and music quarters.

We had resumed having tea with Miss Wilming. She did not speak of the Wings although the inconvenience they had caused would have merited some direct remark from her. As the subject seemed taboo with her I never mentioned the couple from Hong Kong. Despite her calm now she had earlier shown such fear that I did not wish to stir what was evidently unpleasant to her, and still less did I want Philip to develop a panic at the real or imaginery threat of being kidnapped. By having me move in with Philip and entrusting me with a gun Miss Wilming had indicated that she considered kidnapping a real enough threat, yet she had not told me so and, fortunately, she had not spoken of this to Philip either. The Wings had not seemed to me people who would wish to harm the boy. Miss Wilming tended to have exaggerated apprehensions about him. Yet her speaking to the Chief Constable and the presence of Constable Barr and the dogs were evidence that she had taken her fear of the Wings seriously.

Because of her heart-condition Miss Wilming lunched

and dined as seldom as possible with others, but Christmas Eve and Christmas Day were exceptions. On those days we dressed for dinner, and assembled in state in the official dining-room with Skinner enjoying the bringing-in of an important wine to which Philip and I paid full honours by ending up tipsy.

A couple of hundred years earlier the masters of Vrede and their guests had no doubt ended up drunk under that same huge polished table, so in a mild way the last male Wilming was upholding the tradition.

He looked quite comic with his vivacious mahogany face as he spouted at length about Jellyroll Morton, whom I'm sure Miss Wilming took to be a painter. But he was dignity compared with myself, alas! I woke up with an urge to go to the toilet and instead of switching on the light flopped out of bed and into my shoes. That very instant there was a flash as blinding as lightning, a strong smell and the windows shattered.

I stood horror-stricken, a hand on the table, expecting to crumple up. Then I felt no blood trickling and I was still standing in the dark. At last my brain told me I had not been shot at.

The strange thing was that the whole house was still and peaceful — not a mouse stirring, Philip soundly asleep in the next room despite the gun's going off like a cannon, and no Skinner appearing on the scene.

But from below there was the most unignorable barking of foaming-mouthed German shepherd-dogs. I heard them all the more clearly as one of the big window-panes no longer stood between me and the night air.

The bullet, which I had released with my big toe against the trigger had nicked a foot of the bed and then smashed a window. A big one too which would be expensive to replace, and my shoe was ruined.

Constable Barr's voice, in command and V.C.—like, could be heard below. I switched on the light. I was reluctant to appear but at last I went to the window, not leaning too far out lest Constable Barr in his youth take me prematurely for an enemy.

'I'm sorry, Constable,' I said — and it sounded weak and unconvincing — 'I had a slight accident cleaning my gun.'

'At this hour?' came back his disbelieving voice.

'A touch of insomnia,' I faltered above the heads of snarling dogs and the constable.

'I'd take a sleeping pill if I were you,' he said in evident disgust —quite insulting in tone though I deserved it for having raised his hopes of a skirmish. I could never be able to tell anyone I had stood on the gun while going to the toilet; that sounded improbable and fatuous. I would have to pretend it went off while I was cleaning it, despite the odd hour of cleaning firearms, at 3 a.m.

The curtains were blowing into the room, with a singed hole through one of them also. I felt just as I had done as a boy when I fell through a window. Life gets no easier. There was in addition, a terrible freezing draught.

I looked around the room to see if I could find a big board or something to exclude the cold. I could have pinned up one of my blankets, but I needed the blanket. At last I found a big sheet of thinnish brown paper on top of a cupboard, and I pinned it over the window. The brown paper was better than nothing but far from adequate. I needed a screen.

And thus it was that in the early hours and without thinking out the implications of my action I went along to the middle store-room and fetched the kingfisher screen to ward off the draught from the window. By itself the matching box looked so isolated and I could not resist the chance of comparing the workmanship of both items, so I took with me the strange box as well.

CHAPTER TEN

I went to sleep with the determination that I would get rid of the accursed gun at the earliest possible moment, but thanks to Skinner the problem was promptly solved in the morning. He simply took out the bullets, and I put the gun in a drawer.

He also solved the problem of the glassless window. A new sheet would be put in and if Miss Wilming asked she could be told that the glass had suffered mishap while I had been trying to open the window. My reputation as a dauntless marksman and intrepid gun-toter need suffer no diminution. Skinner himself was nervous of the murderous things. As for Philip, I would take no ridicule from him who had peacefully slept through the gun's going-off only a few yards away.

As I woke up, the sight of the kingfisher screen held me entranced. In nature the blues of the kingfisher are eye-taking enough, but in an artifact those blues against the silver lacquer of the river held me a prisoner of their loveliness. There were at least three tones of blue — the sharp rich shade which can be known only as kingfisher blue, then a paler shade of this on the top shoulders of the wings and finally, in mid-wing, a sparsely spotted green-blue. In Japanese all three shades would have come under the generic blue ('aoi') but in English the last shade would have been rather called a green. The artist must have spent considerable time in studying kingfishers, but despite his study he had achieved a simple boldness suggesting the bird in flight.

There was something not quite right, though, with the kingfisher on the box. But as I began to sense this Skinner arrived and for the present there was not time for a longer scrutiny.

Before the end of the year we had a fall of snow — one that did not last long enough to lie deep but fell thickly enough. I would have been sorry to have been at Vrede without seeing snow in the park. This frozen flowering, the Springtide of ice and air, put me in an ecstasy of delight. Chinese poetry is full of snow-descriptions, and comparisons with salt, rice and white petals abound, but the actuality of that fast eye-lash-like dawdling of the flakes to the ground and surfaces is too beautifully delicate for any language, though some of the finest poetry in English and Chinese is about snow. It is a poetic vision itself — an attenuation of matter that from a dusky sky brings purity and spirituality. It obliterates the coarseness of colour, though any colour that is still revealed, like the fire of the holly-berries or the blue of the kingfisher screen against the white-swirling window, is enhanced by the contrast.

When the sky is hard with frost and the stars cluster in festal magnificence then the whiteness of winter is truly a bridal white. But white in China is a colour of death, as befits a winter.

This fall of snow, however, was unfortunately not long lasting. The next day the shapes of cut paper in the shrubbery and woods had drooped and melted into the dun and green of commonplace trees again.

There was another celebration at Vrede on New Year's Eve — the staff had a dance, and at midnight with all the outside lights on, the bells of the chapel struck twelve and Barry the man-servant who had black hair and was swarthy was admitted to bring in the luck. That meant more drinks all round and it was not till the small hours that most members of the household went to bed.

The merrymaking had come to an end. With the first day of the new year we resumed our usual routine of lessons.

The January cold seemed to afflict Miss Wilming. She was in semi-hibernation so that we did not meet her regularly at tea. When we did, I was conscious of Skinner's reference to her heart-condition. Her quiet face with the darkness under the eyes and the slow effort in her least gesture confirmed that she was not in perfect health.

January the seventeenth was a quiet day like any other — a dullish day, and after a final game of ping pong with Philip I settled in bed with a lurid science-fiction paperback that Skinner had recommended and lent me.

I liked to do a spot of not too strenuous reading while Philip soothed himself to slumber with his transistor's Radio Luxembourg, as he did nearly every night. I couldn't really sleep till he had switched it off, though he had it tuned very low. In a way the lowness of volume was more of an irritation as I couldn't hear the tunes properly and as a result my ears were baffled trying to identify the sounds. Surely there was no more need for us to be sharing his rooms now, I thought. At the first chance I would suggest going back to my own bedroom.

I didn't read the science-fiction for long as Philip put off his radio early and I couldn't see what Skinner had found admirable in a story that had decidedly more fiction than science. So I dropped off to sleep.

I was awakened by a bump from the ceiling. It was a sound unlike any other — such as a bird trapped in a chimney or a piece of old timber stretching — that the ear could conceivably experience in an old house on a winter night. It was not repeated.

Because of the wretched book Skinner had lent me, I suppose, a thought of Martian invaders came to me — and then I switched on the light.

No plaster had fallen. There was no hole in the roof. To be safe, I looked in on Philip and saw his sleeping face.

Yet the jolt on the ceiling, which was directly under the roof, had been severe. The nights of Anne Gibson's suicide and the Wings' attempt to climb the wall revived in my mind. I took the revolver, now emptied of its bullets, from the drawer and went into the corridor, switching on the lights as I went along. Ahead of me the Long Gallery was in darkness. The entrance to the pitch-black cavern looked sinister and the gallery was a perfect place for an ambush, for to put on the lights I would have to enter. I halted, uncertain what to do, and opened a window to attract from out of the darkness the attention of Constable Barr and the dogs. There was not a sound from the wretched animals and no sign of Constable Barr. I closed and locked the window again, and ventured into the Long Gallery. Before my hand touched the light switch I was aware of the cold fresh current of air coming to me along the corridor. I switched on the lights and around me was the gallery, as still and vast as usual, but the blowing freshness told me that all was not as usual.

I saw myself being shot down and then ruthless intruders speeding to overpower Philip with no one in the house aware of what was happening. I should have telephoned to Skinner before I left my room. Or, if I now took the chance of reaching the stairs ahead, I could go down to the floor below and find my way to a telephone or the stairs to the servants' quarters.

Not for the first time I cursed the lay-out of this enormous house where one could die trapped like a rat while those on the floor below had to run through room after room to reach a staircase.

With the lights full on in the Long Gallery I opened a window in the hope that Barr's attention if he looked towards the house would be drawn, then I went on, with the useless revolver in my hand.

On the other side of the Long Gallery I turned on the upper floor's last set of lights. I was near the landing at the top of the stairs. The cold air was entering for now there was a large gap in the roof — a square of night sky instead of ceiling. With no attics and lofts at Vrede, the entry to and from the roof was direct at this point, by means of a grooved lead trap. But according to Skinner this approach to the roof was not used, as the trap had been sealed down to make the roof at this point watertight.

As I watched, a ladder that had a familiar look lowered itself steadily till it touched the carpet of the landing. Not the same ladder that I had seen inside the wall, for it was much longer and was an extending one, but of the same lightweight material. Mr. Wing had been proud of the original Hong Kong design.

I waited till he had descended and his sister was coming down the ladder. I presumed the figures were the Wings for both were dressed in rather elegant deep-red running track-suits and their backs were towards me.

'Mr. Wing,' I said, 'I fear I must ask you to return by the way you have come as unauthorized visits are not welcome here, especially at this hour. Surely your previous reception made that clear?'

'You can believe me,' said Mr. Wing, 'when I say that we would both prefer a less athletic and more normal approach

in our visits. Miss Wilming is the one responsible for our
coming the way we do.'

'I fail to see that,' I responded.

'We have repeatedly tried to contact her. Our solicitors
have done everything possible to try to obtain an interview
with her for us. But she has ignored all letters. When we did
get to see her she was not alone and was clearly unwilling to
allow any discussion of our reasonable request.'

'But breaking and entering is not reasonable, not in this
country.'

'We would prefer a conference without heat and an
amicable agreement, but while Miss Wilming persists in
her present attitude of not hearing us at all what other
course have we?' asked Mr. Wing.

'Mr. Wing,' I said, 'before long others will be here. The
police are on the premises. If you go quickly now, at once, I
shall convey what you have said to Miss Wilming and do
my best to get her to agree to a meeting with you for
discussion. I don't know how you have evaded the dogs, but
if you withdraw at once I'll do as I have said and see if Miss
Wilming will not contact your solicitors immediately.'

Mr. Wing motioned to his sister who ascended the
ladder.

'Very well then, I accept your assurance. We have come
by helicopter.'

'Rather an expensive means, surely?'

'Money does not matter so long as we succeed in our
purpose,' said Mr. Wing, nimbly ascending the ladder with
a flash of the smart gold watch on his right wrist.

As he was drawing up the ladder I called out, 'Would
you replace the trap securely?'

'Certainly,' said Mr. Wing, and the trap was shifted and
stamped into place.

I switched off the lights and hastened to close the window
in the Long Gallery. As I did so I heard the helicopter
starting up on the roof.

There was not a sound from the park. I wondered if Mr.
Wing with Hong Kong subtlety had managed to dope all
the dogs, or were they of their own accord having a good
doze on this freezing night? And where was Constable Alan
Barr?

I was glad to get back to bed for my feet felt frozen. But I was unable to get to sleep again at once since for all my calm in Mr. Wing's presence, I had been full of apprehension and now felt like a snapping bow-string. I would have welcomed a large whisky but had to be content with two Phensics. If nights like this occurred often at Vrede (thought I) Miss Wilming won't be the only one with a heart-condition.

CHAPTER ELEVEN

I woke up in the morning with an overhanging sense of something unpleasant to be done. At breakfast, I wrote and gave Mrs. MacDonald a short note for Skinner requesting him to arrange a meeting with Miss Wilming sometime in the course of the morning. I added that the matter I wished to speak about was important.

While I was in the old nursery with Philip, Skinner came to tell me that Miss Wilming would see me in her sitting-room at eleven.

Leaving Philip with some work, I went down to Miss Wilming's quarters at the time appointed. So far I had never entered the rooms that lay to the other side of the entrance hall and had earlier been occupied by her parents. All the rooms led into one another without corridors — bedrooms, dressing-rooms and bathrooms. Into the first, a mixture of sitting-room and private study, I now entered. After the rest of the house the room looked rather plain since it was without vase, painting or any embellishment except a red and white tear-off calendar, but it did hold a comfortable couch to which Miss Wilming bid me while remaining seated in one of her favourite French silk-backed chairs. Her transistor radio was on the mantelpiece, and there was a bright fire.

I did not wish to upset or antagonize Miss Wilming at the very outset so I opened by saying that I had come to fulfil a promise, and then (at first omitting details which might have caused her concern) I explained that Mr. Wing had spoken to me last night — at Vrede.

This startled Miss Wilming. I said that Mr. Wing had spoken to me from the roof and had been in a position where he could easily have attacked and overpowered me and seized Philip if that had been his intention, but he had done none of these things. On my asking why he came clandestinely to Vrede he had told me that Miss Wilming's refusal to answer his solicitor had been the prime obstacle. But on my saying I would try to persuade Miss Wilming to contact him through his solicitors, Mr. Wing had gone away peacefully.

'All he wants,' I concluded, 'is a chance to confer in a friendly manner with you. He does not have hostile intentions.'

'That is what he may profess,' said Miss Wilming sharply.

'I feel I may be intruding on private ground,' I replied, 'but Mr. Wing and his sister do appear to be honourable people. And I promised that I would ask you to consider his request for you to get in touch with him through his solicitors. I am sure that no harm is intended to Philip. Otherwise last night the Wings had ideal conditions to kidnap him.'

I knew that despite my holding the gun I must have looked as nervous as I felt, and there had been opportunities for the Wings, if so disposed, to disarm me by a leap from the ladder or another ruse.

'Their interest does not seem to be in Philip at all,' I concluded, 'let alone harming him.'

Miss Wilming sighed. 'Perhaps I have been in error. I certainly thought that the Wings intended me harm. I am by no means convinced that they do not still intend so. And, of course, harming Philip or holding the threat of doing so over his head is the easiest way of hurting me.'

'But why should the Wings wish to hurt you? You must allow, Miss Wilming, that had they meant to kill you they could have before now achieved that easily enough. They did not speak of you in a way that implied hurt, or make threats.'

'I assume,' said Miss Wilming, 'that they must be actuated by motives of revenge. There is your answer.'

'Revenge? Then you did them some harm?'

'Not I ... My grandfather,' Miss Wilming answered.

'But in the modern world! Grandchildren are unlikely to avenge their grandfather by an attack on someone entirely innocent.'

'They are Chinese, and I do not know how they feel,' said

Miss Wilming. 'If they did not come here for purposes of vengeance, I have no idea why they did come. And is the idea of revenge so very odd when Europeans like the Italians of the South are still swayed by such considerations? From the first time of Mr. Wing's appearance here I expected that he would attempt to take my life or the life of someone related to me. That, of course, could only be Philip.'

'But if there were grounds for your expecting to be murdered, Miss Wilming, the police would have at the least warned the Wings to keep away. You could have been given every protection, instead of one constable and the dogs. You would have been justified in making every protest.'

Miss Wilming sat in thought a minute before commenting: 'Though I had apprehensions of an attack on myself by the Wings, I did not make a formal complaint to the police because there were matters I did not wish to be made public. I feared for Philip. His life has not been smooth. He is impressionable. A disclosure not shocking in itself, but made at the wrong time could bring him much upset — given his nature. And, Mr. Catlow, I did prefer the past to be buried.'

'The Wings, then, have come out of the past?' I asked.

'Very much so. The revelation of our family skeleton cannot possibly hurt anyone except Philip. He is the only one living who is at all concerned. That is why I am puzzled as to the Wings' motives in stirring up memories of old unhappy things. What can they want except a belated vindictive blow at the sole survivors of the English branch of this family?'

'You've said it concerns Philip?'

Miss Wilming sighed once more. 'Indirectly, yes. You may well be a better judge of what concerns him and his reaction than myself. The best thing I suppose is for me to tell the story of a secret in our family, and then you can judge for yourself, and help me to judge, whether I should get in touch with Mr. Wing's legal representative.'

My curiosity by now was aroused so I naturally said nothing to dissuade Miss Wilming from telling me about a chapter in her family history that involved the Wings. But Miss Wilming was not ready to begin her narration at once. She proposed that after lunch we meet again in her sitting-room (with Philip safely set to prepare lessons upstairs) and then she would tell me the story that I hoped would explain the appearance at Vrede of the Chinese brother and sister.

CHAPTER TWELVE

As you know (began Miss Wilming after lunch) the family
came over from the Netherlands with William of Orange
and already in the early eighteenth century they had
shipping interests in Asia. But the expansion of British
interests in the Far East, especially in China and Japan, in
the second half of the last century allowed the firm of
Wilming and Osborne to reach a supremacy in shipping.
Before the airlines you can imagine that the firm had an
almost monopolistic prosperity. Part of the firm's success
was undoubtedly the custom for the elder son of each
generation, once he had sufficiently mastered the business,
to superintend in person and reside in Hong Kong while the
father would then come home permanently to Vrede. This
has gone on for some generations and but for my father's
having only a daughter the custom would have continued to
the present day. Perhaps in due course Philip will live there.
  The family had its villa in Hong Kong, one of those
colonial-style old residences in which the white aristocracy
or élite are accustomed to dwell, and for which there is now
such a demand. Rose Lodge has been inhabited by
generations of my family and of course it is still in my
possession, but now it is occupied by the director of
Wilming and Osborne's in Hong Kong. My great-
grandfather may have loved Rose Lodge. But for the
generations after him, Rose Lodge, despite the charm of the
place, had an inescapable association of misfortune. These
old mansions of Western merchants in the East have a
melancholy all their own, something to do, no doubt, with
the transience of foreign residents, settling with their
fireplaces and apparatus and foreign plants from a
cherished far-away, in a land that will outlive them. Vrede
was our true home. To Vrede we always returned. Yet each

elder son of the family could expect to spend twenty or twenty-five years of his life in Hong Kong — those, too, the years of his prime.

My great-grandfather lived for thirtyfive years at Rose Lodge — he was very much in love with the place, and, being one of those energetic nineteenth century characters, he was even more in love with the risk and adventure of business life. He turned Wilming and Osborne's into an empire. He quitted Rose Lodge and Hong Kong only after he had been paralysed by a stroke.

Thus it was that my grandfather was forty before he went to take over the business and live in Rose Lodge. The change may not have been to his taste. After Cambridge he had settled at Vrede, and nearly twenty years of civilized living with hunting, riding and close social intercourse with the county families had given him a taste for an English existence. He had not long been married and already had one son — my father.

My grandmother Esther was a Stoughton by birth. Her accomplishments were water-painting, singing and playing the piano, and she was proficient in French and Italian. The Stoughton family seat is Exeter Castle and the Stoughton males were accustomed to entering politics. Stoughtons were in the cabinets of both Lord Palmerston and Lord Derby. By the standards of the day Esther had married beneath her in entering a merchant family, however long established and rich. The choice was her own, and she was the virtual mistress of Vrede. An alliance between our family and the Stoughtons was naturally advantageous to us at a time when overseas trade and shipping stood on such a close footing with politics. I have seen a photograph of my grandmother in her last years, but I would not have known her beauty as a fairly young woman except for the portrait of her painted before she left for Hong Kong. She was certainly a beauty (or the painter a great flatterer). She had the most lovely shoulders. I don't think the painter was a flatterer, for the face has too much character. There is nothing demure. It is very much a real face. She looks a lively woman, vivacious, astute and used to having her own way. Her hair in the painting is a torrent of silky black though, of course, in the photograph I saw of her it had turned white.

She had beauty and force of character, and she was prepared to give up the comforts and delights of English society to reside with her husband in Hong Kong. She could not know what sorrow she would bring on herself by quitting Europe.

We look upon things rather differently now when the English-speaking world has other centres, but in my grandmother's time London was like Versailles. Those with country houses in Norfolk were not so far from the centre of excellence, but the further one went from London, to the outer regions of Canada or Delhi or Hong Kong, one could expect only diluted weaker versions of English society — rather like New Zealand today. Esther with her Stoughton background must have possessed an unusual independence of mind to tolerate living in a pastiche of English society at a place like Hong Kong — all the more so as she was devoid of missionary tendencies.

I doubt if Chinese was much studied in the nineteenth century except for trade or conversion. Legge, for example, was a missionary. Anyway, Esther announced her intention of learning some Chinese but any good effect this intention might have made in evangelical quarters in Hong Kong was countered by her expressly not wishing to have a missionary as teacher. She would learn Chinese from a Chinese, and what is more she chose to study not with a Chinese lady, as would have been proper, but a Chinese man. Moreover, he was not a Chinese man of advanced years with a classical beard that would have lent an air of respectability to her studies. The Governor's lady, a cousin of Horatio Bonar, called on Esther to remonstrate about the unseemliness of a lady's learning Chinese at all and especially from a Chinese man.

But since my grandfather had introduced the Chinese man to my grandmother, the female busybodies could not do more than tut-tut among themselves and categorize her as unconventional.

On her arrival in Hong Kong Esther had been eager to acquire some jade — ear-rings and a necklace. I have the pieces yet, though I have never worn them. My grandfather rightly pointed out that the buying of jade is full of risks for an amateur. There were not so many deceiving imitations as now, but the quality of genuine jade varies enormously and the price must be haggled over so that a Western buyer is best accompanied by a knowledgeable Chinese when purchasing expensive jade. My grandfather suggested that a Chinese gentleman Lin Liang Wing, whose family had for long had business dealings with Wilming and Osborne's and who had the reputation of a connoisseur of jade, should accompany and help in the purchase. My grandfather was detained from accompanying Esther so that she and Lin Liang were together at the jade-merchants, choosing the necklace and ear-rings. Esther mentioned her inclination to learn some Chinese, and Lin Liang volunteered to be her teacher.

The sepia photographs of the time, with their poker-back postures, are a poor guide to people's expressiveness, but there are descriptions in letters about how Lin Liang appeared. He wore white silk suits and was something of a dandy. When he met Esther he was twenty-nine and a father. His wife did not move among Westerners. I understand that a man as dashing as Lin Liang, in the full vigour of youth, would not be confined to his home attachments, though the family was all-important. But as long as outside amours were not too costly or likely to injure the paramount family interests, such associations were tolerated.

The truth is that in all cultures love is universal. Confucianism no more than Christianity condones romantic passion which is destructive of family order. When Esther began to study Chinese with Lin Liang, no doubt she had as little foreknowledge of the outcome as Paolo and Francesca when they first opened their books.

Esther had accompanied her husband to Hong Kong fully prepared to be the loving wife, there, as at Vrede. But in a different climate under changed conditions characters change. My grandfather now had to sustain the responsibility of a large firm. His attention was not always on his wife as in the first years of marriage. The climate in summer was a strain so that to her he often appeared to have no longer the attentiveness to which the first years of marriage had accustomed her.

Perhaps my grandfather did in truth neglect her, under the stimulus of a new environment. Perhaps from an increasing familiarity with his nature Esther was becoming disenchanted. Such shifts and changes in relationship are, if not inevitable, common enough. Human personalities are in perpetual transition and adjustment.

Lin Liang provided Esther with new interests for he had the run of the Chinese world about which she was curious, and would devote time to taking her and her son by boat among the islands.

My grandfather William took Lin Liang's attendance on Esther for granted. Wilming and Osborne's was a powerful firm and to him it was natural that a Chinese man in business should try to ingratiate himself by constant small personal services. My grandfather would not have considered it possible that an Englishwoman could ever prefer a Chinaman to a white Christian like himself.

That, however, was what Esther did.

I do not condemn Esther, Mr. Catlow, because, infirm myself, I cannot throw the first stone. I do not know the inner circumstances and I think it improbable that a woman of Esther's intelligence would have embarked on a course of inevitable destruction (in those times) without anguish at foreseeing the circumstances and without the certainty that her love for Lin Liang was worth kin, country and child.

The errors of the heart lack enormity to me because they bring their own inescapable suffering, and they are not earth-shaking evils like intolerance and fanaticism that bring down whole communities in war and destruction.

I do not know if misfortune might have been averted by my grandfather's taking Esther with him on the journey he took to Shanghai, Nagasaki and through Japan to Yokohama. Such a break from Hong Kong might have given Esther time to reflect on what would be the likeliest outcome of her new love.

But he was eager to make the journey as a bachelor in the company of like-minded business friends. A husband's conquests outside marriage were, of course, accepted and sanctioned in practice by the general social code of the day. Poor goose Esther was not to be allowed the same sauce as the gander.

My grandfather set off with his three business associates. He was to be away three months.

The tulip-magnolias smouldered in the garden. The sea like blue tiles trembled in heat before the hills of Hong Kong. This season of early summer Esther was to associate with her 'marriage' to Lin Liang. Usually after he had left in the last hours of the night she would stroll in the dawn-garden hearing the first songs of the birds.

Esther was helped in keeping her love-affair a secret from the other servants by her personal maid, a Devon girl.

I suppose that to enjoy the happiness of the present she closed her mind to considerations of the future. Lin Liang had thought of taking her to Soochow or moving with her to Kobe, but these were dreams. Wilming's was such a well-known firm that the presence of someone like Esther could scarcely be kept secret wherever she fled with her lover, and apart from his family-clan Lin Liang had few resources. As outcasts together I doubt if they could have established a life anywhere in the world at that time except, possibly, Paris. But they dreamed their vague dream of a future together and lived the enchanted present.

I said before that I didn't condemn Esther, but I meant rather that one tends to pity selfishness and weakness when it comes in the guise of love. But the selfishness of both Lin Liang and Esther was evident in that if they had ever succeeded in achieving a life together the cost would have been the disruption of their two families. But what actually happened was worse.

My grandfather William returned to Hong Kong unexpectedly early — almost a month before time. Though he had arrived after midnight, he spent some time drinking with his fellow-travellers before going on to Rose Lodge. It was about four o'clock as he approached.

No one heard him — he was trying to be as quiet as possible so as not to wake up his young son in the hot night. He went towards the sleeping quarters and entered his wife's room.

What he saw there made him rush back to the luggage he had set down. Esther tried to lock the door on him while Lin Liang trying to get out of the window struggled with the mosquito screens. My grandfather threw Esther back and with the Japanese sword he had brought back as a memento he leapt towards the figure at the window. The moonlight flashed in the sword's blade. Lin Liang broke down the mosquito screen but the sword had gone through him. My grandfather followed him. The recognition of Lin Liang's face increased his anger. As Lin Liang strove to carry himself across the garden, my grandfather grabbed him by the hair and as Esther screamed at the window he brought down the sword and severed Lin Liang's head from his body.

My father, then a child in his cot, and the maid from Devon were roused by the screams. The maid seeing what had occurred kept the Chinese servants away by saying that the master had returned unexpectedly.

My grandfather had the maid bring a horse quickly to the side entrance. It was still dark. He set off with the decapitated torso still flowing with blood intending to cast it onto any waste land or the nearest water.

On return he had the blood washed away or covered with soil in the lane and garden. The maid helped him as she was terrified lest he now turn on Esther and her as he had done on Lin Liang. While my grandfather was out, the maid had cleaned and hidden the sword. She dreaded not only that on return my grandfather might use it on Esther but that Esther might turn it on herself.

Esther had been shocked speechless and was now lying as if without sensation on the bed. My grandfather finding himself at the start of a new day had his usual English breakfast prepared.

A week later William and his wife left Hong Kong with their son and the maid for England. Prudence was William's motive for the departure; he could not be sure that Esther in her despair might not blab about what had occurred and provoke a scandal. About the killing I cannot suppose that William, despite being a nominal Christian, felt any shame or remorse. Killing a Chinese man or a dog to him was the same, since neither had souls and a man found in adultery in any case, by his values, deserved to die. William felt no contrition but he wished to avoid publicity.

Back in England Esther was virtually a prisoner at Vrede. You know how on this floor there is no corridor to the rooms. Esther had the rooms behind these and so her whereabouts could be effectively controlled by her husband.

William's withdrawal from Hong Kong was explained by his wife's languishing health. She did not take part in social life, unlike William who was to become quite popular in the county and very fond of hunting.

Esther confined in her rooms with the few objects that had come with her from Hong Kong discovered that she was pregnant. Up till the time of birth my grandfather could not be certain that the child was not his. When Esther was delivered of a male child, my grandfather went to look at the infant. The baby had the little black so-called Mongol spots, which vanish a few days after birth, and this rather than the epicanthine fold and dark eyes since many babies 'look Chinese' at birth told him that the father of the child was the man he had killed. William never had an interest in this second son, who bore the family name, but both sons were sent to school at the earliest possible age. At least to my scoundrel of a grandfather's credit he did not murder his wife or the son she bore another man, but this was probably because of the difficulty in getting rid of them without bother to himself. He took as his mistress .a lady from Ludlow, and on the death of Esther eight years after the return from Hong Kong he made her his wife. This marriage was childless.

My father Edward was brought up to be — and in fact in time became — the heir. But the second son was never asked again to Vrede after the death of Esther. He settled and worked in London, and received an allowance for life on condition that he kept away. By the time my grandfather died, his second 'son' had grown used to living apart from the family he had been born into. He was the grandfather of Philip.

With his second wife, the lady from Ludlow, my grandfather did visit Hong Kong again, but it was not till my father came of age and had married that the tradition came into its own of the eldest son spending his zenith years in the colony. I was born there.

Esther would have been forgotten and never mentioned but for her having had a child whose existence was a fact that could not be brushed away. I used to wonder about my mysterious 'cousins' whom I never saw.

My father, who did not get on with his father's second wife, was told the story by the maid from Devon, and before he died he narrated it all to me.

We had no contact with the Wing family. You know that

the family names of the Chinese are very few in relation to the immense population, and Wing is a common enough name in all conscience. Then over a year ago came a letter from a Chinese legal firm in Hong Kong making an oblique but obvious reference to the murder of Lin Liang by my grandfather. The message was on behalf of the present young generation of Wings. I was very upset because bringing up this ancient unhappiness seemed to be an implied threat to Philip.

Despite the grinding taxation in this country, Mr. Catlow, I do think that from my childhood there have been some substantial improvements in the conscience and humanity of English people. At least, I hope so. As a girl how often did I hear the remark — and I recollect, very clearly hearing it used at a tennis party in Cambridge of a very pleasant young man from Mauritius by an army officer — 'He has a touch of the tar-brush.'

In Islamic civilizations one does not hear such brutally ignorant contempt for mixed ancestry, and how much more tolerant than us are the Portugese in these matters. But today in Britain what would it matter that Philip's great-grandfather was a Chinaman, Lin Liang, and not a Dutch-descended Englishman? Not that I wanted the family skeleton out of the cupboard, of course. My real fear was not that the Wings meant blackmail but that they wanted to extract money by kidnapping Philip. Among the Chinese in Singapore and Hong Kong wealthy families have a lively dread of kidnapping as it is such a common practice. Philip is so frail too.

'But he has an underlying toughness,' I here put in.

I didn't want him to go through a deeply upsetting experience (Miss Wilming went on). But if kidnapping is not in the Wing's minds, what do they want? It does seem odd indeed that they should seek vengeance or retribution or satisfaction now for an injury done to their family so long ago. At least such a motive is odd by occidental standards. But if the Wings do not want vengeance, what else could they possibly want?

'Miss Wilming,' I put in, 'the best thing would be to reply to their solicitor and ask him just that.'

'Do you really think so?' she asked doubtfully.

'I do indeed.'

'And you don't think Philip will react badly to finding out his great grandfather was Lin Liang and not William Wilming? Strictly speaking, he has no Wilming blood at all.'

'But you and he are both descended from Esther. I don't think it will matter a damn to him, begging your pardon, about who his great-grandfather was. What do most people know about their great-grandfathers? Philip and you remain as closely related through the female line. He might be upset if he suddenly found himself without known family, relationship, but that is not the case.'

'No — I see what you mean. Would you write to the solicitors then for me? I'll show you the letters. I would feel awkward in replying now after ignoring their approaches.'

So I looked at the letters and then wrote a short note which I signed. Miss Wilming approved of what I had written, and the following was then sent off:

'Miss Wilming has asked me to let you know, in response to your earlier communications on behalf of Mr. and Miss Wing, that she is prepared to listen sympathetically to any representations Mr. and Miss Wing wish to address to her. But such representations must be made in a reasonable way, and all unauthorized visits to her property must cease.'

CHAPTER THIRTEEN

An immediate result of my easier relations with Miss Wilming, after her confiding family secrets to me, I plucked up courage to suggest that she provide Philip with a horse for exercise. I pointed out that the park was ideal for riding.

Miss Wilming got in touch with a riding stables and Mrs. Parker turned up with a graceful chestnut mare and instructed Philip how to manage it. There was also a large amiable grey for me — a retired cart-horse ponderous in locomotion, for which I was grateful, though its size made me nervous about being stepped on.

If encouraged, Mrs. Parker could have been a bit of a bore for she took riding so seriously. Philip did not aspire to be a jumper — Miss Wilming would have fainted. We wanted to make use of the park, and riding was both an accomplishment and a means of health. As later, he would no doubt drive a car, there seemed no point in training like a Mongol archer.

I found Dobbin an excellent mount, cautious when there was a mole-hill in the way and fond of pausing to examine wild flowers in case they were edible. She was never disconcerting — in short, a reliable and mature being — and with her size I had the sensation of being a rajah seated on a mighty sacred elephant. Our strolls around the park gave me a good appetite for supper. I often wrote my letters while on Dobbin's back. Watching Philip with glowing face as he rode his horse, I looked to the years ahead when his children would be playing in the park. Already I could see in Philip a sketch of the shy slim undergraduate to come — the chrysalis of awkward boy would change to a competent manhood. I did not see how any after-effect of Lin Liang's brutal death could mar the emerging of Philip's life. All that the old unhappy love-disaster had left as legacy was the tint of brown eyes and glossy black hair and the more delicate build of body which had struck me in Philip when we first met.

In the midst of our excitement with the horses there came a response from the London solicitor of the Wings. He wrote to say that Miss Wing had been injured while motoring in France and that her brother was with her. But Mr. Wing had sent word that he was gratified by the communication from Vrede and as soon as circumstances were more normal he would get in touch with Miss Wilming.

This news of an accident to Miss Wing caused Miss Wilming some worry but the solicitor had not given details or the exact address of the Wings, so it seemed that matters might have to rest for a time. However, thinking the matter over to myself, since Miss Wilming had expressed concern, I suggested that we ask the solicitor for Miss Wing's address. On receipt of this Miss Wilming had flowers delivered by Interflora to Miss Wing at a nursing-home in Rouen.

In March Miss Wilming strained her heart through moving a typewriter. I remembered how astonished I had been when she summoned Skinner to turn the hands of the clock. But I had not known then of what she and Skinner called her 'heart-condition'. All her sitting down and slow sedate ways were attributable to this. She referred once to the constant nagging pain in the top of her arm and the tightness in the brain which followed any excitement. She had moved the typewriter in sheer unforgetfulness and dizziness, palpitations and fainting were the consequence. The doctor told her that she must avoid exertion of any sort in future but endeavour to take gentle exercise. Miss Wilming was now well aware that a normal life, one of hazard, upset and excitement, was beyond her capacity, but her wealth and the isolated placidity of Vrede could yet secure conditions allowing her years of life. But she attended to some matters in her will, the solicitor coming to Vrede. When she did leave her bed, she moved from room to room with the aid of an ivory stick.

With the brightness and flashes of warmth now that Spring had arrived I sometimes liked the windows opened. Moving to and from them I found the kingfisher screen inconveniently placed. There was not so much need now, when the view from the windows was a living picture, to gaze upon the brilliance of an art-object, and I feared that the screen which I had moved without permission might get damaged with so much movement by it. So I took it and the matching lacquered box back to the store-room and left them there covered up.

CHAPTER FOURTEEN

I was awakened by a heavy thumping on the door. As I was going to open it I saw that the time was only half-past seven. Philip in his pyjamas appeared from his room at the moment I unlocked the door and found myself confronting a policeman.

A policeman is always an upsetting sight — from childhool I had associated the police with death, disaster or arrest — and without preparation to see one right in front of me so early in the morning in the corridor of Vrede made me go weak at the knees. This one had eyes like a seagull's.

'The inspector asks for you to come down to the library,' he said.

'I haven't had a cup of tea,' I croaked. My head swam with possible misdeeds — unreturned library books, the time on the bus when no conductor had come to collect my fare, or the incident with a jazz musician under Morecambe Pier — (the tide out).

'There's hot coffee in the library,' spoke the policeman with what I sensitively took to be a tinge of contempt for my less-than-steel-like civilian comportment.

'Never mind,' I said to Philip. 'You try to sleep and I'll bring breakfast when I come back.' My voice faltered on the last words as it suddenly occurred to me that I might not be coming back.

'Can you tell me what this is about?' I managed to ask with revived dignity as I put on a dressing-gown. After all, there was no need to summon me or anyone at this gestapo-like hour.

'I am not at liberty to answer,' said the policeman freezingly. 'Would you please stay in your room?' he addressed Philip.

I glimpsed Philip's surprised still sleepy face as I padded

off, Seagull-eyes looming in blue and silver at my back.

Outside the library Skinner and Mrs. MacDonald were seated. Mrs. MacDonald had her hair in a net and Skinner was unshaven, as I was myself. The pair of them looked like derelicts who had been sleeping on park-benches all night. As I was shown into the library I had an impression that something was missing in the corridor.

'Mr. Catlow,' intoned Seagull-eyes, and my pleasure at being still 'Mr.' was reduced by memories of *The Times*, using that polite form of sentenced criminals.

I was handed a cup of coffee (though it was tea I craved) and the inspector with awry eyebrows and a disconcerting stare sized me up.

'I am not at my best,' I thought fit to point out.

'Your looks are not relevant to this enquiry,' the inspector crushed me. 'We allowed you to sleep on. But perhaps now you're here you'll tell me what noises you heard during the night.'

'What sort of noises?'

'You tell me.'

'I can't say that I remember any noises at all.'

'No noises,' said the inspector sceptically. 'Are you a heavy sleeper as a rule?'

'Inspector,' I began, taking a warmer interest in that I now had to discuss myself. 'The only pattern to my sleep is that I find it murder to get off and murder to rouse.'

'Why do you use the word "murder"?' he pounced.

'It's a natural word to use, surely?' Meaning "extreme difficulty". Why else should I use it?'

'I am asking you questions,' said the inspector, and it's odd you should bring in murder when you are asked what sounds you heard in the night.'

'I heard none I told you.'

'Though on previous occasions, I am told, you were as sensitive as a hare,' he said with what sounded like a sneer.

'I am not acquainted with the nervous structures of hares. Nothing disturbed me last night.'

'Were you drugged?'

'Drugged?' I echoed.

'Yes, drugged. What did you drink before going to bed?'

'I drank a pint of Ovaltine. I find it helps me to sleep.'

'Who prepared it?' he relentlessly pursued.

'I made it myself, with some for Philip. We had some toast with it, spread with marmite.'

He tchaed.

'I didn't put any drug in my own Ovaltine,' I pointed out. 'It would spoil the flavour.'

'What else will explain your not hearing six men in the corridor outside?' he asked.

'Six men?'

'Six intruders. Yet you say you heard nothing. Come, Mr. Catlow.'

'Some nights I sleep better than others,' I heard myself saying weakly. 'Not that I would have slept if I had known there were intruders about. I am rather nervous — at least I was, in the winter.'

'If you're nervous, what difference does the season make?'

I tried to pull myself together and dispel my morning muzziness. The inspector and I were not communicating. Was he really too thick to understand that winter in a large lonely mansion was inevitably more eerie than the same place in the friendly Spring? I ignored his comment.

'Try to remember,' he said lighting a cigarette, 'whether you heard anyone speaking Chinese in the night. Did you?'

'No. As I've already said I heard nothing at all. Had I heard any sounds, I would have gone to see, or called Skinner. I do think, inspector, you should tell me what happened.'

'Miss Wilming is dead,' said the inspector, watching me as he smoked.

I was too shocked to exclaim. After a while I asked: 'Her heart?'

'The doctor thinks so — from shock. She had been robbed.'

'I hope you realize,' I said somewhat angrily, 'that her nephew, or second cousin, her only English relative, is upstairs, a sensitive boy — and I trust you don't intend to break this news to him as you have done to me.'

'I intend to ask you to break the news to him,' said the inspector.

I digested this.

'I suppose they were very close?' asked the inspector in a kinder tone.

'No — no,' I said slowly. 'At least, an outsider can't judge when there is such a divide of generations. But they were the only blood-relatives each had.' I thought fleetingly of the Wings who were also blood-relatives. 'In England that is. There is an elder branch of the Wilming family in Amsterdam. But now Philip is left without family. He was isolated enough before.'

'Is there any reason why he can't be at school?'

'He is the sort of boy who would be isolated at a public school ... But I agree with you that the right sort of school would have been best.' I was not going to tell the insepctor about Philip's bed-wetting.

'Well, he'll be the heir now,' the inspector commented.

'I expect so.'

'I'm afraid I must ask you, Mr. Catlow, not to leave the estate. This is a very curious case, and we think someone on the staff must be involved. A considerable amount of jewellery and objects of all descriptions have been taken, and Miss Wilming died when surprised by intruders. You will appreciate that investigations have hardly started and we would welcome your co-operation. No doubt you will be wanting to go back to your pupil. I'll have breakfasts sent up to you. You'll find that the entire telephone system inside and external has been put out of action.'

All this was rather much to take in first thing in the morning — my employer dead and the house robbed, with the Wings, the only Chinese-speakers that were likely to be involved, suspected of being the villains. Outside the library Skinner managed a wintery smile as I passed, but Mrs. MacDonald was evidently past emotion. The constable stood there to make sure that we did not communicate, so I trailed back through the house to Philip. I dreaded having to tell him that his aunt was no more, especially as it was on the death of his mother that Miss Wilming had brought him to Vrede. I decided not to say anything until after breakfast, when I would feel better able to handle the situation.

Philip just looked solemn when I told him. I was not able to gauge any deeper reaction. By sparing him at all costs the nightmare experience of looking at the dead in the coffin I thought he would not take his bereavement too much to heart. The natural excitement of the robbery, with its real-life mystery, diverted his attention to some extent.

Normally so quiet, the house was now in chaos with all the visitors — the police were permanently on the scene, but the undertakers, the clergymen who held the services in the chapel, Miss Wilming's solicitors, telephone men and press-reporters also appeared. Amid all the disturbance I kept Philip to a skeleton time-table so that we lived in some order. Once meal-times were regularized and we were in communication with the servants, we were able to gain some idea of how the robbery had taken place.

The intruders in a vehicle had entered the park by the side-gates. This had meant their coming past the farm. None in the family there had heard anyone passing, just as well for their own safety. The telephone wires to the farm had been cut. The fact that a large van had been able to drive so close to the farmhouse without anyone hearing was suspicious in the view of the police and the family had been exhaustively questioned. To bring them more under suspicion, the padlock on the gates had been opened with a key.

The van had then been driven across the park to that side of the front terraces furthest from the rooms occupied by Miss Wilming, and the intruders had then moved on foot to the front door which was so seldom opened. They must have been carrying equipment with them for these burglars were evidently the products of British education's increasing stress upon technology. Or perhaps they had profited in their humble way from the James Bond films. They had progressed beyond the jemmy stage. Some of the guard-dogs had been laid low with hypnotic guns. Constable Barr, not having been roused by any barking, had been taking a kip during the time he should have been vigilant; the Spring night and a bottle of Guinness had been his undoing. In any case after months of inactivity he had no reason to suppose that that night would be different from any other.

But the intruders with their equipment more bang-up-to-date than the manufacturers of Vrede's burglar-alarm system had worked on the front door and immobilized the alarm-device with which it was fitted. Then they had opened the ancient door and simply walked in. They had put the telephone system out of action and removed from the house whatever they desired. From the discrimination of their choice the police believed that the gang were connected with dealers specializing in oriental antiques. As yet the full extent of what had been taken was not known for the family collection at Vrede had not been catalogued. Nevertheless, many items had been listed or discussed in works by experts; and Skinner was helping the police to locate those places that indicated a significant absence.

None of the servants had been roused. Philip and I had heard nothing. The robbers presumably wore noiseless footwear and worked with speed and precision, removing the stolen objects to the van with deft organization and logistical expertise.

They had erred, however, in entering Miss Wilming's bedroom to take her jewellery. However light-footed and adroit the entry, Miss Wilming with her weak heart had been the one person in the entire house to be roused from sleep — and the shock of seeing an intruder, or intruders, in her room had killed her. An autopsy had been performed on her body; had marks of violence been found, the police would have been able to make more serious charges against the thieves. The possibility of murder had not been ruled out.

The jewellery that had been taken had been kept in the dressing-room next to the bedroom. Had there been a corridor on that floor the thieves could have gone directly to the dressing-room without entering the bedroom and Miss Wilming would have been spared the scare that cost her her life.

How the police were progressing in their investigation was unknown to us. But I was asked to step down to the library again and answer some further questions of Inspector Hussey. I took it that he had been talking with the Chief Constable and learnt from him that Miss Wilming had been disturbed at one time by the presence of Mr. and Miss Wing.

I certainly did not want to pass on the old story of Esther and her Chinese lover as it seemed to have nothing to do with the present robbery, but by not doing so Miss Wilming's earlier consternation at the appearance of the Wings at Vrede was left unexplained.

'Miss Wilming and Mr. Wing were corresponding with one another,' I told the inspector. 'He and his sister were to come here but Miss Wing was injured in a car accident at Rouen, and that is where they are now.'

'And what was their relationship with Miss Wilming — business?' asked the inspector, not so innocently, it seemed to me.

'Well, not quite. The Wing family have been in Hong Kong for generations, like the Wilmings, and there was a business relationship between Miss Wilming's grandfather and the Wing's great-grandfather ages ago, so there was a sort of traditional sentimental tie. It is natural for Mr. and Miss Wing to be interested in this history of their own family and so in an English lady whose own family history crosses theirs. There is new interest in Hong Kong about the early days of the colony.'

'That doesn't explain Miss Wilming's being frightened,' the inspector pointed out. 'She asked for a police constable to be stationed here.'

'Miss Wilming was very timid,' I said lamely. 'I mean — she took alarm easily about things that didn't need it. This I thought was due to her heart-condition that made her exaggerate some matters. I don't mean that she wasn't brave. I don't think she foresaw, despite the alarms and that, anyone would really come here and steal so much Chinese stuff. That wouldn't have worried her. What she would have worried about was anyone's harming Philip.'

I saw that the inspector was impressed by this last remark. 'Had she any reason to fear for his safety?' he asked.

'No — but she always worried about Philip. That was why she asked me to move nearer to him. This fear of hers about Philip's safety and the robbery do seem to be quite different things, inspector. For if there had been any connection Philip wouldn't be here now, would he? He would have been kidnapped.'

'Instead he has come into a fortune,' stated the inspector.

'I hope so, for his sake,' I said. 'At sixteen he would be very unqualified to manage on his own.'

'Anyway, he slept right through it all, according to you,' said Inspector Hussey.

'I hope you aren't meaning he went down and frightened

his aunt to death. I may have been asleep, but if Philip or anyone else had come into my room I would have heard — especially Philip. He crashes into everything. Ovaltine may help me to sleep,' I concluded with dignity, 'but it does not render me completely paralysed and unconscious!'

And so my second interview with the inspector ended.

I suppose I can call the walk I took with the inspector through the rooms, while he pointed out what property had been stolen, a third interview.

'Of course you know Chinese!' he remarked casually in a statement rather than a question.

At this I understood that he had been checking my background and that I was under suspicion as being the thieves' inside accomplice. I had not mentioned my year's crash course at Ealing to Miss Wilming because it had seemed irrelevant. When I came to Vrede I had not been aware that the Wilming family had connections with Hong Kong.

'A year's crash course does not entitle me to say I "know" Chinese,' I told the inspector who smiled as if the point was unimportant.

I was able to describe to him the scroll of the Taoist sage which had been stolen. Skinner had evidently noticed that the scroll had gone but had not been able to give a description of it. I had made a copy of the Chinese inscription and seal and said I would send the copy down to the inspector. He remarked that this would be very helpful when it came to identifying the stolen property, but he gave no indication of how close or not the police were to doing this.

I concluded that Inspector Hussey was turning over in his mind the possibility that the Wings outside had planted a Chinese speaker, myself, inside Vrede to steal a valuable Chinese collection. I wondered if the inspector thought the collection had been moved already to Hong Kong or was on its way there. If the inspector was working on such a theory, then he must be feeling baffled. Why come all the way from Hong Kong to ship back Chinese antiques to China? Such a theory ended in a cul-de-sac.

Anyway, as the inspector didn't, I knew that Mr. and Miss Wing had not planted me inside Vrede.

Neither Skinner nor Mrs. MacDonald seemed to me at

all likely to be in league with a gang. No one in the household did. That left only Constable Barr, who had been strangely remiss and asleep when the intruders were at work. But the Chief Constable himself had stationed Barr in the grounds.

Perhaps, then, there had been no inside agent, but the thieves had appeared to be so familiar with the lay-out of the house.

CHAPTER FIFTEEN

With no Miss Wilming, I felt the monotony at Vrede. At four o'clock each day I was reminded that we could not be asked to tea. Not that Miss Wilming had been a radiant personality, but she was steady and I had grown to appreciate her. The funeral was as awful as most funerals. I was plunged into total gloom and felt bereft of any will to live. The only funerals we enjoy, I suppose, are of those whom we thoroughly detested while living. However, I was prepared. I had arranged an antidote.

I had noticed in the local paper that there would be a one-night showing of the film of Prokoviev's *Romeo and Juliet* at Lytton. I was well aware that Miss Wilming was not likely to have approved without permission of my whisking Philip to a film on the day of her funeral, but I think she would finally have accepted that Philip needed to be diverted. At least I hoped he would be diverted, especially if we stopped in a hostelry afterwards for a quick one, since *Romeo and Juliet* in any form encourages a vivacious melancholy in me — cheerfully suicidal when I am in love, as I was not — and both *Romeo and Juliet* and a funeral in one day might be thought a bit much. But there was no alternative film.

Since I seemed under some suspicion, I thought it would be tactful to mention our absence for the evening to the inspector. Rather reluctantly, I explained we would be seeing a film — 'for educational purposes,' I added.

He gave his opinion that the film would be a bit gloomy and one of the Crazy Gang would have been more cheering, but he offered us a lift in a local police-car and I accepted. I was skipping an evening when I would have had to put in a police appearance among the clergymen and solicitors assembled at the house since the will was to be read the following morning. Byt my first duty was to Philip and the clerical atmosphere was very oppressive for a boy. Archdeacon Baxter did not have a light-hearted nature, though admittedly we were meeting him for the first time at a funeral. But there seemed little prospect that he would brighten at all for the evening.

The first act of the Prokoviev ballet, with the music being unfamiliar and the sets being so brownish, did not excite me, and only with the last two acts did the power of the music and the dramatic dancing bring delight. The performance ended much earlier than I had expected, and having had no dinner Philip and I looked for a place to eat. The hotel in the square had stopped serving meals, but down a side-street I was surprised to spot a small new Chinese restaurant. Not that one should be surprised at the ubiquity of Chinese restaurants, in present-day Britain, but Lytton was such a small place in a so out-of-the-way nook in Norfolk that I wondered how the Lin Hong restaurant could find enough customers.

We had a crab-dish, crab and green peas in an omelette over shredded cabbage, and some lichees. Philip wanted to try some Chinese wine and I thought we might as well have our drinks in the restaurant as go into a pub afterwards.

The Lin Hong restaurant was fan-shaped with the door of dark glass. On each side of the door were windows of the same dark glass hung with slatted bamboo. People in the street could look into the restaurant through the door's dark glass and those inside the restaurant could watch the street. I was startled, when I chanced to look in the direction of the door, to see Inspector Hussey in the dark tank of glass gazing at us. Had he trailed us, I wondered, or was he too just in that street to find somewhere to eat? Or had be found an improbably sinister connection between the Lin Hong restaurant and the robbery at Vrede? The poor inspector seemed to have China on the brain.

'Don't you like the wine?' asked Philip, seeing my face.

'Oh yes — it's unusual. I think I prefer the gold-coloured hot wine.' (We were mixing our drinks with a vengeance as we had decided to sample them all.)

'It's powerful stuff,' said Philip whose face was red.

This was so true that I could not help wondering if I had not imagined the inspector outside.

At ten o'clock the next morning the solicitors began reading the will. As the funeral had taken place in the afternoon, I suppose the reading of the will was put over to the next morning since Miss Wilming's last will and testament had an epic spaciousness. I had been asked to join the group in the library, and I found that I too figured in a small way in the will. Miss Wilming had requested me to superintend Philip's education till he was eighteen years of age (after which he was to be at complete liberty to determine his own course). Archdeacon Baxter and I were to be associated in a general (not financial) guardianship of Philip's affairs. Miss Wilming had not spoken to me of these plans of hers. I suppose that very recently she had come to think that Philip might fare better with some influence from me than put entirely under the Archdeacon's jurisdiction. Of course I was at liberty to refuse, but under her will she had made provision for my staying a further two years at Vrede.

In effect the bulk of her estate went to Philip, but in her munificence to the Church of England Miss Wilming seemed inspired by Queen Anne. There were, in addition, numerous minor bequests, among which I recognized Skinner and Mrs. MacDonald as recipients. With my total ignorance of finance, I had believed that rich families were dying out in England, but, whatever the estate and death duties would be, the Wilming opulence was assumed to be safe for another generation and Vrede Manor not yet ripe for the National Trust. As I listened to the elaborately legal sentences of the will, I thought to myself that some practical economics might well be of more use to Philip, now that he had such a wealthy inheritance, than most university courses. Had Miss Wilming lived, she could have passed on something of her experience and financial expertise to him, for I assumed she had considerable shrewdness of her own and could not be completely dependent on professional advice. Now, no doubt, he would go into the firm of Wilming and Osborne at the age of eighteen, in the London offices if Hong Kong had ceased to be a British colony. The Wilmings had been wealthy before Hong Kong left Chinese hands, and I did not doubt that they would continue so after Hong Kong had returned. Miss Wilming had acquired varied interests in Eire, and she had shares in Swiss and Australian companies. Philip had some business to go through with the solicitors and Archdeacon Baxter was desirous to have a talk with him, so, being on my own, I thought I might take a stroll in the park. I went upstairs to change into more comfortable shoes when, passing the store-rooms, I had an impulse to view the kingfisher screen again. I tried the door of the middle store-room. It yielded.

I saw at once that many of the boxed scrolls kept there had disappeared. But — what I should have perhaps expected since there had been a large-scale robbery, but came now as a shock — the kingfisher screen was no longer where I had left it, and the matching box had also gone.

CHAPTER SIXTEEN

I told Inspector Hussey about the disappearance of the screen and box and as I was able to give a complete description he took notes and seemed pleased at my help. The theft of the kingfisher screen made me indignant; I had loved it and presumably had I kept it in my bedroom it would never have gone. Miss Wilming's jewels I had never seen and I could not really grieve for them, but I felt grief at the loss of the screen. In an over-warm atmosphere the lacquer would be so easily damaged, and the screen was unique, quite different from the coromandel screens from China which are so common in the West.

As I spoke with the inspector, I recognized whom he resembled and why he had awed me so much. He had the manner and the look of my old headmaster — a nervous haughtiness with the occasional attempt at dropping into familiarity, on my lower level, which never succeeded. Remembering all the long-loathed misdeeds of my old headmaster I snapped rather viciously at the inspector for tailing me and Philip to the Lin Hong restaurant.

The inspector was so taken aback and blushed so obviously that I felt ashamed of my fierceness. After all, he was not my former headmaster and should not be discomfitted for my pedagogic past.

'The two affairs have nothing in common, Mr. Catlow,' said he, 'except the Chinese element, which may be accidental. I shouldn't tell you but we suspect there may be an opium joint run by the proprietor of the Lin Hong.'

'An opium joint in Lytton!' I exclaimed.

'I don't know why you should despise Lytton. It is a township with many traditions,' said the inspector huffily.

'Oh, I don't despise it. I am so surprised. Lytton is full of surprises. If I had known opium was available, Philip and I would have had a puff after the lichees.'

'I must remind you he is a minor.'

'Inspector Hussey,' I explained patiently. 'That was a joke.'

'It does not do to make jokes to the police,' said the inspector, so solemnly that I was in doubt whether he was pulling my leg or really meant it. I was not likely to attempt any further humour with the police as they were constantly at Vrede and seemed so serious and single-minded that I was acutely conscious that I was considered not above suspicion. Skinner and Mrs. MacDonald felt as uncomfortable, and I suppose the only ones at Vrede to derive delight from the police presence were the kitchen maids who flirted with the young constables drinking cups of tea and having pieces of pie in the kitchen when their superiors were not around. According to Mrs. MacDonald the female staff had become uncontrollable. Cupid wearing blue had landed in the Vrede kitchen.

I would have liked to move back to my own part of the house but to my surprise Inspector Hussey thought I should continue to keep close to Philip. I felt a bit like one of those Egyptian slaves who were buried with their monarch. The inspector evidently thought that kidnapping was not entirely out of the question now Philip was rich in his own right. Constable Barr was no longer in the grounds at night but we had other policemen. This was near the time that Philip was to sit for his 'O' levels, as I pointed out. Inspector Hussey thought that Philip might as well travel to the examination centre in a police car.

'I don't know how he'll ever grow up to live an ordinary normal life if he takes his 'O' levels flanked by policemen,' I grumbled.

'You told me last week that nobody was normal,' retorted Inspector Hussey with his more than elephantine memory.

'I did?' I queried.

'You did. I made a note,' stated the inspector.

'I wish you wouldn't make an issue out of everything I say. Fancy making notes,' I protested.

'You say some remarkable things,' said the inspector.

'Well, I don't know that I do,' I replied irritably. 'Not that anyone has recorded my conversation before — when I said that nobody was normal, inspector, I must have overlooked you — you are a painfully literal man.'

'Conscientious,' amended the inspector.

'Metaphorless — a man without metaphors.'

Philip did go to sit for his 'O' levels in a police car.

While Philip was at his exams I had plenty of time to brood about my future. Considering the low level of intelligence of most educational bodies I foresaw that I would do my future no good by staying a further two years at Vrede in privately coaching Philip for his 'A' levels. Two years in an educational establishment would look more solid on paper. Educational boards like their papers to be filled in a regular approved fashion. But I decided that I would never apply for a headmastership. I would let my life move as it and I pleased. Perhaps Philip should go to a school — I must have a talk with Archdeacon Baxter — and then if I stayed at Vrede as the will provided, I could plunge deeper into Chinese and perhaps make a much needed inventory of the Chinese works of art there, all that had not been stolen. But what school was there that would give Philip the companionship and stimulus he needed? There would be some. But the final choice must be his. If he did wish to stay at Vrede, then I would coach him here as best I could. But, in my opinion, what he needed above all else was a group of co-evals. Males are not meant to develop alone, though they certainly don't all need rugger.

After the examination Philip was in no mood for any more sustained study for a while, so the days passed in an orgy of listening to music and playing poker. I did not know how to play poker, and never became much good at it, but Philip had learnt it at school and so, when the weather was rainy, we had sessions of poker and I lost continually. Skinner got drawn into a few games and scooped the winnings from Philip.

I was conscious that Archdeacon Baxter would not have approved and that bridge or whist would have been more socially acceptable accomplishments for my pupil to acquire. But I took his poker-mood as a temporary and inevitable reaction to the examinations, and the cigarette smoking likewise. The denseness of the smoke wafted from his room made me cough, though he seemed to think I could not smell the strong aroma. Mrs. MacDonald at first complained that the inspector (she supposed) was emptying all the decorative boxes holding cigarettes for guests. These boxes were strewn about the rooms and as there had hardly been any guests to help themselves some of the cigarettes must have been lying in the boxes for decades. In replenishing the guests' cigarette boxes Mrs. MacDonald discovered that the current cigarette packets contained coupons, which she began collecting to obtain a hand-bag.

In this anarchic post-examination time I received a letter from Mr. Wing and the solicitors forwarded to Philip one which they had received from him.

The letter to me was informal. Mr. Wing wrote that he had been grieved to hear of Miss Wilming's sudden death. He had hoped to discuss a certain matter with her, but as this was now impossible, he hoped that he could call at Vrede and talk instead with the new owner of the property. He trusted that I would help him. He and his sister were now in London and anxious to come to Vrede for a talk.

The letter sent on to Philip was one in reply to the solicitors' that informed Mr. Wing Miss Wilming was deceased. Mr. Wing asked that he be granted an interview with whoever was now in possession of the Chinese antiquities and art objects at Vrede.

The decision was now up to Philip. He was unaware of his own connection with the Wings, and the Wings were seemingly unaware of the treasures lost by theft at Vrede. I had an idea that Inspector Hussey would be interested to know that Mr. and Miss Wing wanted to visit Vrede, and I was very curious myself to learn what they had wanted to ask Miss Wilming and now Philip.

Naturally Philip welcomed the idea of acting as host, and Mr. and Miss Wing were invited to Vrede during the following week, on the days most convenient for them.

I mentioned to Inspector Hussey that the Wing brother and sister would be making a visit.

'I knew they had returned to England,' he said. 'But I didn't know they were coming here.'

'It has only just been arranged — By the way, they do not appear to have heard at all of our burglary.'

'That will be a surprise for them then,' said the inspector.

CHAPTER SEVENTEEN

Philip as the head of the household took his duties as host seriously enough to consider entertaining the Wings with a Chinese dinner, and Mrs. MacDonald was given a few books on Chinese cooking, from the library, to take down to the cook. That evening Mrs. MacDonald reappeared to say cook had looked at the books and if it was all right with Mr. Philip she would prefer to follow her own lights.

'Her own lights? What does she mean by that?' I put in.

'I don't think cook feels up to it,' said Mrs. MacDonald. 'In fact she's ready to give notice. Miss Wilming never complained. Good English cooking satisfied her, day in day out. Steak and kidney pudding was her love. Wanting heathen dishes makes cook feel slighted. I don't think you should have sent her those books, Mr. Philip. Cook's always been one to follow her own lights.'

'Yes, really, the Wings aren't likely to relish what the English think are Chinese dishes,' I said, 'especially cook's version.'

'I wanted something especial,' said Philip obstinately. 'Aunt Wilhemina was very stodgy in her tastes.'

'Mrs. MacDonald,' said I, 'couldn't you flatter cook into doing something especial and going a bit mad — what about a whole roasted young pig? I'm sure the Wings would like that. Or roasted swans?'

'Roasted swans!' exclaimed Mrs. MacDonald. 'Roast and eat such a beautiful bird! Cook would never contemplate it.'

'Well, I'm sure cook could do something dazzling and flamboyant if she set her mind to it,' I said.

'Mr. Catlow,' replied Mrs. MacDonald, 'cook's very sensitive. Any suggestions about a change she takes as a criticism.'

'But we've never had Chinese guests before,' Philip pointed out.

'Cook said she was born an English woman and she'll die one.'

'Then we'll have the wretched steak and kidney pudding,' said I in disgust.

'I'm sure I'm only reporting what cook said,' Mrs. MacDonald replied in stiff tones.

'She must have something unusual in her repertoire,' Philip took up. 'After all she's a qualified cook.'

'The Brighouse Girls' Domestic Science Diploma with a distinction,' exclaimed Mrs. MacDonald.

'So I'm sure she'll think up something out of the ordinary for Mr. and Miss Wing,' ended Philip.

'Then I'll tell her you're leaving it to her imagination,' concluded Mrs. MacDonald.

'But try to insinuate a whole young suckling pig done in cider into her mind,' I shot at Mrs. MacDonald departing.

'You've such wild ideas, Mr. Catlow,' said Mrs. MacDonald from the door.

Our attempts to brighten the Vrede cuisine for Mr. and Miss Wing foundered on cook's traditionalism, but by the time the guests arrived she had been brought round to accepting a recipe for roast pig from the Philippines which she had read in a woman's magazine.

We had been looking forward to the guests arriving, I also from curiosity to know what the Wings had wanted to discuss with Miss Wilming, but I had not been without some anxiety since Philip did not know that he had Chinese blood from his great-grandmother's love-affair with Lin Liang. I could not see that this would have much effect on him since only with budgerigars, race-horses and royal houses do the details of pedigrees generations earlier count for much. But what, I wondered, if Philip was proud of being a Wilming, 'the last of the Wilmings,' as his aunt had so dramatically stated, and now was to learn that strictly he was not a Wilming at all?

But her second son had been born to Esther in England, after she had left Hong Kong hastily with her husband, and so the Wing family might never have known of or connected the new baby with their murdered kinsman. If Mr. and Miss Wing did not know of Philip's distant kinship with them, then all would be well. Philip could go on undisturbedly believing he was a Wilming.

When Mr. and Miss Wing arrived, I noticed at once how Miss Wing had improved in appearance. Despite her accident, she had gained from her stay in France; — her dress-sense had improved enormously, and instead of plain natural skin and eyebrows she had applied make-up, lavishly but to delightful effect, and had pencilled thin half-moons. Mr. Wing looked just the same as ever but one hardly noticed him now that his sister in a dazzling brocade white dress with flashing nails and blue eye-shadow hit one's sight like a bomb. Miss Wing, I thought to myself as I observed her new poise and happiness had found romance. She could not have changed so much for the better simply by being in a French car crash. Of course, politeness demanded that we should commiserate with Miss Wing on her recent dreadful experience, but her radiance and maturing beauty made our sympathy sound ridiculous. Philip sat open-mouthed. Since the inspector was still using the library as his headquarters, we had gone into the music-room and had tea. Miss Wing chatting away poured out the tea. On the last occasion Miss Wilming had done the honours and Miss Wing had been shy, silent and rather like a plain severe student.

It was left to me to prod Mr. Wing about the purpose for which he had come to Vrede. I simply stated that he had had some matter which he wished to discuss with Miss Wilming.

Mr. Wing's face clouded. He looked uneasy and his sister lost her smile.

'It is a business of some delicacy and may be long in the telling. And I am working only on a hypothesis. Perhaps this evening we can get down to talking about it. Now that we are here I find it uncomfortable to plunge at once into such an unhappy affair.'

'Well, we can talk after dinner,' I said. We fell back into the easy chatter of tea-time, though I remember briefly wondering to myself whether I should mention to Mr. Wing that there had recently been a serious robbery and at that very moment an inspector was at work in the house. But Mr. Wing obviously wished all serious matters to be kept till after dinner.

CHAPTER EIGHTEEN

The dinner was badly balanced with the main dish the exotic Philippine pork and pineaples and everything else, from the Windsor soup to the custard, rampantly English. Miss Wilming had not entertained much, and cook was certainly a strong reason not to.

After dinner we moved to the powder-blue drawing room, even though the inspector had quitted the library and the house. By locking the far door we were secure from interruption, and after the coffee Skinner was told to keep the nearer door closed. The powder-blue drawing room had been rifled in the robbery and there were obvious gaps — at least, to the eyes of those accustomed to the room. The silk on the wall was much brighter where a nineteenth century oil-painting of Hon Kong harbour had hung, and seeing Mr. Wing looking that way I explained that there had been a robbery and Miss Wilming had in fact succumbed to a heart-attack while the thieves were in her room taking her jewels.

Mr. Wing said he was sorry to hear it; he had not realized that Miss Wilming had died as a consequence of a robbery.

'No violence was used. Miss Wilming's heart was weak, and the shock was too much,' I explained.

'But how terrible for you all,' exclaimed Miss Wing. 'Poor Miss Wilming. She was such a gentle lady.'

There was a silence. I asked Miss Wing if she minded Philip and myself smoking, as I could see Philip half-fainting from lack of nicotine.

'I'd like a cigarette myself,' said Miss Wing briskly. 'I didn't dare to light up last time as I thought Miss Wilming would not approve.'

I passed the box of cigarettes around. Mr. Wing declined

politely but firmly: 'I disapprove of the habit.'

'Oh dear,' I moaned since the smoke was already swirling about Mr. Wing's head and good manners demanded that we should not poison a guest.

'Take no notice of Ah Yuk,' intervened his sister. 'He always makes a fuss of being such a model of virtue. Actually he is, but at times it can be tiresome.'

Mr. Wing grinned.

Eventually when we were all settled, I hinted that Mr. Wing might like to broach the matter for which he had been so keen to come to Vrede. He looked a bit discomfited and began with a long hesitant 'Well.'

I thought he was never going to start and his sister must have thought so too for she said encouragingly, 'Don't be so nervous, Ah Yuk.'

'It's difficult to know where to begin,' Mr. Wing complained. 'But I'll plunge right into the matter and explain about my great-grandfather. He was a very handsome man, and in character he was extremely amorous. He was very astute also, and he certainly did not fritter away the family fortunes because of his affairs. But he brought disaster upon himself all the same. He was a remarkable man. The Western powers had begun their colonial exploitation of China and in his lifetime Hong Kong passed into British hands. This meant that great-grandfather Lin more than any of his ancestors was to encounter — and a little more than encounter, — a range of blue-eyed beauties. My great-grandfather was an innovator, a pioneer, a trail-blazer. Perhaps he was the first man in China to fall in love with the wife of a barbarian who came not from the Steppes of Asia but from far over the sea. Yes, he fell in love with a blue-eyed woman.'

'Excuse me,' I put in, 'but Mrs. Wilming, your great-grandmother, Philip, was certainly not blue-eyed. She had brown eyes.'

'Not blue-eyed!' Mr. Wing exclaimed, put out by my interruption. 'But all the English have blue eyes.'

'Not Mrs. Wilming,' I stated firmly.

'Yes, Ah Yuk, all foreigners do not have blue eyes,' Miss Wing corroborated.

'I am astonished,' said Mr. Wing. 'But I am glad if the lady did not have blue eyes as then great-grandfather's taste cannot be considered as having a flaw. Blue eyes are frightening and animal-like. I have often wondered how he could bear to look into them in bed as he must have had to do.'

'He could have worn dark spectacles, of course,' said Miss Wing gravely. Her brother looked at her crossly for this flippant observation.

'But if she had brown eyes, then I can see to some extent how he could have become attracted,' Mr. Wing went on. — He was infatuated with Mrs. Wilming. And great-grandfather Lin was so handsome and engaging that Mrs. Wilming naturally was filled with passion for one so different from her long-nosed red-haired husband who thought only of making money. Ordinary people at that time could not understand a love like theirs, but those who reflect deeply see the strange destiny that was at work through history and the rise and fall of empires to bring together from the ends of the earth two whose lives and backgrounds had been so dissimilar. But the destiny of lovers is all the more tragic as the love is deep. Love is an excess; lack of moderation brings inevitable retribution. Our great-grandfather despite his charm and many abilities was to perish young. The husband returned unexpectedly one night and surprised his wife and Lin Liang in bed together. As my ancestor tried to escape the Englishman threw himself on him with a sword and cut off Lin Liang's head.

'What I have to tell you next comes from the traditions of our house. My great-grandmother had been aware of how matters stood between her husband and Mrs. Wilming, but she had been helpless, and since she loved her husband had not sought the assistance of her brothers.

'But then came the morning of the tragedy. An old serving-woman who had once waited on my great-grandmother happened to be looking out of her window at dawn when she saw the rich Englishman come riding up. She watched him as he heaved the naked body of a man and threw it into some water. Then the Englishman rode away. The old servant asked a friend to help and the two old women went to the water's edge and looked, then between the two of them they managed to bring the pitiable headless body to land. Of course they could see that the murdered man was Chinese, and though the body was headless yet the Englishman had made a mistake. To stop the flowing of the blood where the head had been cut off he had attached cloths, and one of these was a torn garment of Lin Liang's that bore his family crest. No doubt the emblem was meaningless to the Englishman, but the old woman recognized the crest of our family and she was certain that the murdered man was no other than Lin Liang. There was no head. At no time had the old woman seen the Englishman disposing of a head — merely the body.

'Between them the two old servants hid the body in the shelter of a shed and wrapped it in clothes. They did not want the vengeance of the English lord to fall on them, but they knew how under the English there was no just law for the Chinese and that a man like Mr. Wilming could murder as he pleased. Finally, the old servant went to the elder brother of my great-grandmother and told him of all that she had witnessed and her belief that the murdered man was Lin Liang.

'Our great grand-uncle was a person of ability and he acted promptly. He went to inspect the body, and recognizing his brother-in-law had the corpse conveyed to a fitter hiding-place, and members of his household traced the fast-vanishing and in part already obliterated trail of blood to Rose Villa.

'No doubt my great grand-uncle planned or wanted to plan a terrible revenge upon Mr. Wilming, and since there has never been any revenge we of the present generation should inherit that debt of vengeance. I had an idea that Miss Wilming feared my sister and I had come to Vrede with motives of revenge for this long-past wrong. But such were not our intentions. Over the ages, in the context of human history, wrongs reap their own harvest of bitterness, while like an echo the reverberation grows less with time. Besides, for a person of moral sensibility the chain of causation is extended by the satisfaction found in revenge — freedom from evil comes when the heart no longer remembers resentments or triumphs. But, naturally, my great grand-uncle was too near the horror and injury to be so detached. Whatever revenge he hoped, he could not achieve it for immediately, as it seemed, Mr. Wilming with his wife and child left Hong Kong for their own country.

'Now, my great-grandfather, Lin Liang, could not be

properly laid to rest in the ancestral earth when his body was in two parts and one part was missing. His spirit had been affrighted out of his body, and was he to have the additional humiliation among the ghosts of having a body only partly buried with full rites? To this day the body waits in Hong Kong till his family restores the head to it. When that is achieved the departed can rest in peace.

'As I told you, the old servant-woman saw that the horse-rider brought a body but no head. As the murder was so recent and had taken place at Rose Villa, our family and my great-grand uncle had the grounds of Rose Villa and every inch inside it searched time and time again. Miss Wilming might have been surprised to hear how often her family property in Hong Kong had been combed through. We knew, too, the exact route taken by Mr. Wilming when in the early hours he set out to cast away our ancestor's headless corpse. But no head was ever found.

'Our father was a man of wide reading and good deductive powers, and he thought out a theory which explained why the head of our unfortunate ancestor has never been found in Hong Kong. Remember, that in addition to the old serving-woman's testimony and what our family had uncovered for itself there was also information given to our family by the Chinese servants employed at Rose Villa. By thinking on this accumulated evidence my father concluded that the head might have not been found in Hong Kong simply because the head was not in Hong Kong. The Wilmings had left Hong Kong by the first ship.

'My father pieced together what he thought had happened. Mr. Wilming had left Rose Villa and taken the headless body with him. Perhaps he thought the head was too risky because too obvious a means of identfication and he intended on return to bury or dispose of it. However, on leaving Rose Villa the two women, Mrs. Wilming and her maid, found themselves alone. The Chinese servants had been excluded and told to keep away, and since they suspected what was occurring they were afraid to venture among the Europeans.

'Esther Wilming found herself left with the severed head of the man she loved — and the maid. Well, the maid could have taken the head away, though if she did she certainly found a perfect hiding place, for the skull has not been found yet, and, remember, all likely places near Rose Villa were searched repeatedly over the years. The other possibility is that Mrs. Wilming, seeing the chance to protect and cherish the relic of her lover from the madness of her husband, secreted the head somewhere. On the husband's return the maid would tell him that she had already disposed of the head.

'Now among all the records handed down to us we know that Mrs. Wilming possessed a late Ming screen with a design of kingfishers. When she left Hong Kong she took very little with her from Rose Villa — in fact she took nothing from Rose Villa except this kingfisher screen and a box, made at a later date to the same design. She was a woman who must have felt distraught at what she had been through, and yet she arranged, while otherwise taking only her clothes and personal possessions, for the screen and the matching box to be shipped to her in England.

'My father spotted the significance of the box. He considered that the head of our ancestor had been guarded and taken to England in that box by the woman who loved him.'

'Oh but the box is upstairs,' cried Philip excitedly.

'No, Philip. It isn't any more,' I said. 'Mr. Wing, the screen and the box were stolen in the robbery.'

CHAPTER NINETEEN

As Mr. Wing was speaking, I had come to the conclusion that the lacquer box, with the kingfisher design was the most likely hiding-place for Lin Liang's head. But since the box had been stolen with the screen and so much else, there was no way to verify the theory of Mr. Wing's father.

I suggested to the Wings that we let Inspector Hussey know that their purpose in coming to Vrede was to ascertain the whereabouts of the kingfisher box, though there was no need to give him the full history of the head in case the box did not in fact contain it. We could say that the Wings were interested in the box as a piece of fine lacquer.

The next morning we told the inspector. Mr. Wing was able to give a completer description of the screen and box than myself — for in the Wing family records the dates and details were more expertly noticed — and Mr. Wing had a long conversation about some of the stolen Chinese objects with the inspector. It appeared — I could not be sure — that Inspector Hussey no longer classed the Wings as leading suspects. He had checked that they had been out of England at the time of the robbery, and now he learnt that the object which they were so anxious to obtain had itself been stolen before they could set eyes on it.

The presence of the Wings as guests was a great pleasure to us. Mr. Wing was an enthusiast for ping-pong and played for hours with Philip, while I strolled in the grounds with Miss Wing, whom I now thought of less as charming than alluring. My pedagogic conscience slept, though at times I felt a guilty twinge when a thought of Archdeacon Baxter crossed my mind. All my pupil was doing was playing pop records and ping-pong, consuming the best port from the cellars and smoking his head off.

Apart from my walks with Miss Wing, I was interested in

questioning her brother about various Chinese art-works which remained at Vrede. The inspector did not object to our now replacing the obvious gaps in some rooms with objects brought down from the store-rooms, and the advice of the Wings about how to set out the art-works to best advantage was much appreciated. Their visit had extended already to two weeks (despite cook's refusal, with the threat of her notice, to attempt something so far out as rice pilaff) and some of the rooms rearranged by the Wing's advice had a greatly enhanced appearance. Of course Vrede was such a patchwork of centuries and countries that homogeneity was out of the question, but in those rooms where the decor and art-objects were Chinese, Mr. Wing could smooth out (to him) obvious disharmonies and avoid serious clashes.

Mr. Wing and his sister were due in Hong Kong by August at the latest and perhaps they would have stayed with us till the time for their departure from England — their errand uncompleted — had Inspector Hussey not proved himself the unexpected possessor of deduction and flair more abundant in the detectives of fiction than reality. We were all taken aback. Skinner was so impressed that afterwards he addressed Inspector Hussey as 'sir', an honour he had made a point of omitting.

I am sure Inspector Hussey had followed so many false trails — for example, keeping the Lin Hong restaurant under observation for possible illicit opium-trafficking — that his achieving a coup probably saved him from premature retirement.

We knew that the police must be on to something the morning that Inspector Hussey requested Philip and myself to step down to the library and he met us with a face as rosy and beaming as a Homeric sun.

'Hitchcock has confessed to being an accomplice,' the inspector said at once, 'and I would like us all to travel to London together to identify the stolen objects.'

CHAPTER TWENTY

To drive to London — the group of us in two police cars — was enchanting. The hedges of may were coming into bloom; the sleek cattle, so substantially English, surveyed us from their vast meadows. Then we were coming into London, our progress slower and slower as we neared the centre, seeing the names of famous streets, and we turned off Oxford Street into a labyrinth of lanes full of attractive small shops and stopped in Beak Street.

I had never heard of Beak Street. It sounded sinister. We were before an antique shop with the name MARKOWITZ above. In the window resting on a flow of crumpled white silk was a single Wedgewood plate, and in a corner of the window was a small printed sign stating 'European and Chinese antiques'.

'The place was raided this morning,' said Inspector Hussey. 'We can miss the shop. I want you to see the warehouse.'

Further along the street was a door that led us into what looked like a workshop. We went upstairs and entered what appeared to be a comfortable office.

'They had a filing cabinet against the wall,' remarked the inspector depressing a catch. A door in the wall slid back and we entered another room. 'Though what use a secret room was to them when anyone made a serious search I don't know. The dimensions of the ceiling below showed there was another place up here.'

'The kingfisher screen!' I exclaimed.

'The box,' cried Mr. Wing, moving towards it.

'Well, I'd like you to take your time and identify as many articles as you can,' said the inspector. 'The identification must be positive.'

'There's no doubt whatever this is the screen,' I said. 'It's even in the original wrapping.'

'The jewels have gone, of course,' the inspector lamented. 'No chance of recovering them.'

'And the scroll of the Taoist sage,' I cried. Mr. and Miss Wing came across to look at the scroll-painting. Philip was meanwhile spotting items that he recognized as having been taken from Vrede.

Inspector Hussey gave us some information about the apprehension of the thieves. The demand for antiques in the United States had made it worthwhile for a gang to pick on selected British country houses and take the cream of the collected treasures. Mr. Cyril Markowitz had assembled a team of cracksmen who all had creditable 'A' levels, and Mr. Markowitz himself had a specialist knowledge of European and Chinese *objets d'art*. He had long cast an eye on the collection at Vrede Manor, one not open to public viewing but known to him from mention in reference works and the occasional loaned object. Vrede had been investigated, but no chance to raid the interior had presented itself till the former lodge-keeper, the surly Hitchcock, had lost his employment and went off with a grudge against the over-rich owner of Vrede.

Supplied with information that the best way into the grounds was through the side-gates by the farm and told about the internal lay-out and security precautions of the house, Markowitz was easily able to organize a smooth break-in and take away some of the better items. His work was all the easier as the objects at Vrede were not catalogued and as traceable as those in a museum. But greed had led him to one disaster — in taking the jewels his men had awakened Miss Wilming who with the shock became the victim of a heart-attack.

The inspector's voice conveyed the deepest regret that he had not been able to hang a charge of manslaughter or even robbery with violence for her death, upon Mr. Markowitz's being charged with twenty years of wilful evasion of payment of income-tax, as documents found in the raid indicated.

'Not just the usual fiddle you expect in business,' said the inspector with sonorous satisfaction. 'The bugger had been doing the country out of millions. The British might have been first on the moon but for the cheating likes of him. He had a yacht and two mistresses and we counted thirty-eight suits in his wardrobe. I ask you, what does any man want with thirty-eight suits?'

'Perhaps he had to look well-dressed in his business,' Philip suddenly suggested brightly, and I was glad he had not voiced what I had just thought — better thirty-eight suits than two suits and thirty-eight mistresses.

'Not at the expense of us tax-payers,' proclaimed the inspector virtuously.

CHAPTER TWENTY-ONE

Regulations did not allow us to take away immediately with us those articles which we knew had come from Vrede. The objects, in any case, required as careful handling in transport as they had received when Mr. Markowitz — a superb art-thief who could claim with truth that nothing he stole had ever been damaged when in his care, unlike what some owners did to their possessions — had spirited them away. So the Wings like Philip and myself had to wait, with the greatest impatience, till the lacquer box with the kingfisher design was returned to us by the police.

At last, there it was, on the library rug, and we would know once and for all whether the head of Lin Liang was inside.

In Markowitz's secret store-room I had noticed Mr. Wing through his big black-rimmed spectacles give the box a look of horror. Miss Wing too had had an expression of consternation on her face. I wondered at the time what had upset them as they knew of course what grisly contents the box might have. Now, in the library at Vrede, they told us.

'You know, the screen is of late Ming workanship,' said Mr. Wing.

'It is very beautiful — with a superb finish,' I agreed. 'I have often wondered whether the kingfisher had a tragic symbolism.'

'Ah,' said Mr. Wing with a sigh, 'there is a feeling about the screen. If we knew its history, why, it was made in the first place and for whom ... There is a gladness about its brightness, but its destiny was to unite it to this box, and the box is of ill-omen. You can see that the craftsmanship of the box is inferior — I date it from the beginning of the Ching. The purpose of the box — well, the years of the Ming overthrow and the coming of the Manchu ascendance were troubled ones for China. Many loyal to the King Dynasty were beheaded. This box was made to carry a head.'

'Whoever had the screen,' explained Miss Wing, 'must have had need of a box in which to hold the head of some relative or beloved one — possibly till times were more settled.'

'So you see,' went on Mr. Wing,' 'the lacquer box had had a history of tragedy and violence before it ever came into the possession of Mrs. Esther Wilming, and for a second time the box was to have a tragic role. It is a box of sorrow. Who knows indeed whether the two earlier lovers of irresistible karma were not destined to return to existence in another age as Lin Liang and Esther Wilming and re-enact their former unhappy passion? Such a strange pattern of fate has involved this box.'

'Cannot we open it?' pleaded Philip, who had all youth's enthusiasm for the gruesome. As Mr. and Miss Wing still seemed to be in superstitious awe of the box, I undertook to do so and my fingers identified where the original lid had closed on to the box. But now it was shut fast.

'I think it has been glued on,' I said.

'Let me prise it open,' Philip suggested.

'You'll break the lid that way. Mr. Wing, wouldn't a sharp knife be best?'

'A sharp knife would do it,' Mr. Wing agreed, obviously finding the moments of opening the box of some emotional weight.

We sent Skinner to fetch a sharp knife, and then we began to loosen the glued lid from the box. Slowly we disengaged the rim of the original lid from the box and tugged it off.

There was a smell of decayed rose-petals, an exhaustion of old sweetness that was not unpleasant. The box looked full of withered brown petals rather like a bowl filled with cornflakes.

Mr. Wing put in his hand and, for a moment, pulled out the mummified head to which the withered petals clung like dead bees. A glance was as much as any of us could take.

When Esther and her maid, working in frantic haste during the husband's absence, put Lin Liang's head in the box, they must have packed it with petals of roses and other fragrant flowers from the garden, and perhaps poured in perfumes — for the library was filled with extinguished sweetness like the last resurgence of love before a final life ebbs into nirvana.

CHAPTER TWENTY-TWO

The Autumn found me alone, without a pupil, at Vrede. I had started work on compiling a complete catalogue of the art-works in the house. Philip had departed for the L W school in Dorset. Archdeacon Baxter had insisted on Philip's going to school, Philip himself wanted to and I thought it for the best. The L W had enough Christian flavour to have the Archdeacon's warm approval; he seemed to think there would be enough cold morning baths, early chapels and rugby to foster a Christian conscience, but Philip and I had visited the school and rather liked the very small classes and the air of comfort. If cold baths did intrude (I told Philip) he could always come home on the next train.

Mr. and Miss Wing had left England with the head of their ancestor. Miss Wing had already written twice to me, and I to her. I hoped that she would come to England again or I meet her in Hong Kong. She was, I felt, a girl who developed her own personality more when away from the authority of her brother. She had begun to flower in France, but how I did not know — in a nursing home with a broken leg perhaps she had met a French doctor who had brought the new life I had sensed in her.

At Vrede I felt I was living with the ghosts of the Wilmings — Esther who stayed in her rooms with the head of her dead lover enclosed in the kingfisher box, Miss Wilming seated in a French chair while the clock rang for tea, old William Wilming going out hunting. Even the stack of pop records in Philip's rooms now had an air of things left behind and ghostly. For what is more fleeting than boyhood?

I loved to go out into the park and smell the real Autumn.

The trees had their wealth of young green acorns, and the fallow deer fled into the flame-like bracken. The house from a distance looked like a Greek temple.

Autumn is oppressive with the sense of all Autumns gone, yet the air is radiant. The birds sing as if mindful of next year. As I walk in the park at Vrede, at every step I wonder at the haunted beauty of England, so old and so young. Under the trees once again I read Miss Wing's last letter.